PRAISE FOR GRACELEY KNOX & D.D. MIERS

"The dawn of a new age of vampire." - **Crafting Geeky Bibliophile**

"*Thirst* is the first in a new series from the writing team of Graceley Knox and D. D. Miers. Whatever they are doing, they are doing it right because *Thirst* had me riveted." - **Tome Tender Book Blog**

"The premise for *Thirst* is so unique... And these aren't just vampires, they are Kresova." - **IB Book Blogging**

"A CRAZY, WILD, INSANE RIDE THAT KEPT ME ON THE LEDGE" - **Marie's Tempting Reads**

"If you haven't read any books by Graceley Knox or D. D. Miers well get busy because you are missing out on two very gifted story weavers!" - **Goodreads Reviewer**

GIRL, VAMPIRE

BOOK THREE

GIRL, IMMORTAL

USA TODAY BESTSELLING AUTHORS

KNOX & MIERS

Edited by: Lorraine Fico-White - Magnifico Manuscripts
Cover Design by: Lori Grundy

To Dee,

You don't know I'm doing this, but I seriously would be lost without you. Thank you for being my crazy idea loving, finish my sentences, love me no matter how insane I'm being, twin.

xx,
Graceley

GIRL, IMMORTAL

CHAOTIC PRESS, LLC

THE DRAUGUR

Long before Vlad the Impaler, there was Vasile Draugur.

Descendant of a warlord emperor, Vasile was a force never before witnessed in history. But for all his strength and power, his people fell into dissolution as famine, disease, and war spread through their land. Desperate and desirous to prove himself, Vasile sought the help of the Servants of Hekate, the right hand to the queen of the underworld.

He begged for help, grace, and mercy, but his cries fell on deaf ears. His fate was sealed the moment he walked into the temple asking for Hekate's help.

Unhappy with their prophecy and angered by the priestess's words, Vasile slaughtered one of Heckate's priestesses, a young innocent who was actually Princess Avilda, daughter of the great King Ivar Baetal.

He attempted to save the girl and failed.

Hekate cursed him with the words, "For the blood you stole this night, you shall live a walking death." Horrified by their leader's actions, Vasile's people rebelled, sealing him in a cave, alone, unable to die, and hungry.

Seeking revenge for the loss of his daughter, Ivar Baetal ravaged the known world, offering his life and his humanity to a witch in order to achieve his goals. Upon capture by a great foe, Ivar ripped out the leader's throat, promising to destroy every one of them. The tale of an undead leader from hell spread like wildfire among those left in the wreckage.

Gathering his forces, Ivar soon believed the myths told about him, drinking blood every night to continue to lead his army to victory and avenge his daughter. Madness took his mind and his own officers turned on him, refusing to drink blood as he did. Though they managed to plunge a knife into his heart, Ivar rose again the next night, declaring himself a god and turning those remaining loyal to him into creatures of his own making—the Baetal. Ivar swore to find the man who took his daughter and destroy any last trace of him and his line.

Years later, an earthquake decimated the cave Vasile had been sealed in, setting him free. Forgotten and unsure of the new world around him, he created others like him, destined to live a walking death. Soon, their numbers grew, and the Draugur were born—powerful, wise, and among the oldest of the ancient vampire races. Unknown to Vasil, his enemy still walked the earth, searching and hunting him.

The Draugur and the Baetal.

They cannot be known.

Be seen.

They live by one rule: Their existence relies on their very nonexistence.

PROLOGUE

Arsen

Nikolai's Lab, Baetal Compound

"Thirty seconds." Jackson says, his eyes glancing back and forth from me to the door.

"I know."

"That door is not going to hold."

"I know, I know!"

"Do you? Do you know that in thirty seconds we are going to be neck deep in murderous vampires? Because you sure as hell aren't acting like it!"

"Just give me a minute!"

Chaos. Blood thunders in my ears, almost drowning out the hammering of fists on the doors, the tearing of metal, the screaming of furious voices.

Sasha is beautiful, even sprawled unconscious on the floor in front of me, bound in silver to keep the virus that's killing her from turning her into a murderous monster. I fumble with the lab notes on the counter, the fiddly little vials and droppers, and the complicated equipment which is all that might save her life. I fight the urge to throw it all at the wall. It might be more useful as a projectile weapon right now.

"Arsen!" Jackson barks as one of the vampires manages to warp the metal doors enough to get its head through. Jackson puts a silver crossbow bolt through it without hesitation, but the others are already taking advantage of the gap. "We have to go!"

"Would you shut the fuck up and let me focus?" I snarl back at him, losing my control and hurling an empty glass vial at one of the vampires trying to claw through the barricaded doors. "She's dying right now, and I can't save her because I didn't pass high school fucking chemistry!"

"That's it," Jackson says and turns away from the door, shoving the crossbow into my hands. "You watch the door."

He drags the notes toward him and examines what I've already done, trying to catch up. He squints, and I can tell he's almost as baffled by the notes as I am.

"Fuck it," he mutters, pushing the notes aside. "It's close enough."

He grabs a syringe and fills it, until I grab it out of his hands.

"You can't do that!" I snap. "You don't know what it'll do to her! What if it doesn't work?"

"Then we'll be exactly as fucked as we will be if you waffle around for another ten minutes and we all get killed!" Jackson says, snatching the syringe back out of my hand.

"I'm not going to let you waste her only chance!" I struggle to take the syringe from him again. Instead he shoves it into my hands.

"Fine! You do it then! Because either way, if you don't do it now, we are all going to die!"

I know he's right even if I really don't want to admit it. I kneel beside Sasha with the syringe, my hands shaking. Lying there, she looks perfect, not like a virus is eating her alive. Like at any moment she'll open her eyes and be normal. It makes it all the harder to use a cure on her that might kill her, or make her worse, or maybe just do nothing at all.

Maybe I should look at the notes again, start over—

There's another tearing metal sound. The doors are about to give.

"Just do it!" Jackson demands. "We don't have a choice! We don't have time!"

I raise the syringe, but I can't bring it down.

Jackson curses. "Fucking vampires," he says, snatching the syringe from me and plunging it into her chest, thumb down. Behind him, the doors finally give and a mob of angry vampires rush at us like a flood.

We kill a lot of vamps. Dumbasses loyal to their clan who don't know that we're trying to save them, too.

I'll feel bad about it later.

One of Jackson's silver nitrate flash grenades buys us enough space to kick out a ceiling tile and drag Sasha's unresponsive body up into the ceiling. From there, we claw our way out of a vent and onto the roof, still followed by a mob of furious Baetal.

From there it's just running. Running and running, and for all of it Sasha hangs limp in my arms. Every minute she isn't waking up, my anxiety grows. She should have woken up by now. I didn't expect the cure to be instantaneous, but vampires are damn fast healers.

She should have woken up by now.

We huddle in a warehouse somewhere while Jackson catches his breath. He's tough as hell, but he's still human. And as much as he would never, ever admit it, I can see the fearful tension in his shoulders as he keeps watch through a gap in the decrepit building's corrugated metal siding, waiting for the Baetal to find us.

"Arsen, you can't do this," he says, not looking away from the gap. It's the third time he's said it since we stopped, and I had told him what I planned.

"I can, and I will."

"You realize this is suicide, right?" he says, casting me a caustic glance. "Far be it from me to stop a vampire from killing himself, but it'll be a hell of a lot easier to get out of this mess with you alive and hauling your own weight."

"I can't let her die," I tell him. It's all I'm willing to say anymore. "I won't."

Maybe it is suicide. But a life without her isn't one I feel like living.

I undo the collar of my dress shirt and unsnap the top three buttons.

"I'm not negotiating, Jackson," I say, and I hope he can tell by the look in my eyes how serious I am. "If you're not going to help, you can leave. I wouldn't blame you."

He takes a deep breath through his nose and puts his cross bow roughly aside.

"In for a penny, in for a pound," he mutters, rolling up his sleeves. "But if you die, I'm taking your boots."

"Deal."

I don't die, but for a while I want to.

During the few hours it takes us to limp home, Jackson supports both me and Sasha and complains bitterly the whole time. It wouldn't have been a stroll in the moonlight even if I hadn't been mostly dead. We constantly stop to hide or take another route to avoid the Baetal. We nearly run into them a dozen times, any of which would have been fatal with both me and Sasha dead weight and Jackson already low on ammo, nursing injuries from the earlier fight.

When I finally lay Sasha down in her bed, it's more than a literal weight off my shoulders. I black out for a blink and slump against Jackson, who diverts me into a chair with a grimace.

"I don't get you, man," Jackson says, shaking his head as I struggle to find my senses. "Is it just a vampire thing or what?"

"What?" I mumble, struggling to stay conscious.

"The two-faced Machiavellian bullshit," Jackson explains, sitting down on the edge of Sasha's bed. "You manipulated her, messed with her feelings, that whole stupid tournament thing, treating her like a prize, making her think you only wanted her for the cure—and then tonight you nearly die for her. A couple of times. What is that?"

"It isn't like that," I say, too tired to feel properly ashamed. "You don't understand."

"You're damn right I don't," Jackson says.

"I love her," I say, trying to make him understand, or maybe myself.

"I don't think you know what love is," Jackson replies, raising an eyebrow. "Cause it sure as hell ain't *that*. You can throw yourself in front of as many bullets for her as you like. If after the bullets stop flying, you're just going to use her, that's not love."

"I didn't use her," I protest, but I can't put any strength in it. I'm too tired and too guilty.

"Sure seems like she thinks you did," Jackson replies. "And I'm pretty sure how she feels about it is what matters."

I close my eyes, too tired to argue or explain myself.

Jackson sighs and I hear the clink of his equipment and the creak of the bed as he stands up. I open my eyes and see him staring down at Sasha, an odd softness in his eyes.

"She's something special," he says, and looks at me. "Not just because of her blood either. If you want her to stay a part of your undead life—assuming you both live, anyway—you'd better stop only treating her like you'd die for her while she's already dying."

He doesn't understand. No one can.

In the beginning, yes, I made a mistake. But after my initial claim, I fell in love with her. The first true emotion I've felt this deep in my gut since my sister's change.

I hurt her.

I lied.

I *used* her.

But in the end, I've never stopped loving her. Even when I knew she might hate me for it. Even when I knew I could lose her for it.

CHAPTER 1

Two weeks later.

I must be dead.

Or *more* dead because instead of feeling like shit, I feel pretty good. Which doesn't make any sense considering my last memories are of me succumbing to the parasite. For a minute, I'm really worried that if I open my eyes I'll discover I'm a mindless monster surrounded by the dead bodies of everybody I care about. But the comfortable mattress under me and the sound of low, peaceful snoring somewhere nearby makes that feel less likely. In which case, I must definitely be dead.

I open my eyes slowly, not sure what to expect from the afterlife. What I discover is my room at the Draugur compound, just the way I left it. The curtains of my window are open on a clear night, crickets singing in the grass. The snoring is coming from a chair to the right of my bed, where a man is reclining, hands on his stomach, hat pulled low over his face.

"Jackson?" I ask, my voice rough from disuse.

Jackson, my best friend and vampire hunter, sits up with an

undignified snort and almost loses his hat. He blinks at me as he gathers himself.

"Holy shit!" he says. "You're awake."

I sit up, my head spinning a little, and look around in confusion. Jackson scrambles to steady me and I ignore him, swinging my legs over the side of the bed.

"What happened?" I ask, confused. "Why am I not dead? Where's Arsen?"

"That's a whole mess of questions I'd be happy to answer if you stop trying to get out of the bed," he says, impatiently. "Please?"

"I feel fine," I say, but bring my legs back into the bed, crossing them under me. "How long was I out?"

"Two weeks."

"Holy crap."

I suddenly understand his concern. Some of the energy I'd woken up brimming with, drains away as I take in the consequences. "Jesus Christ! What did I miss?"

"Nothing good," Jackson admits, sitting back in his chair, expression grim. "We got the lab notes on how to make the vaccine out of Nikolai's lab, but without you to interpret the strange annotations, they aren't doing much good. They've got a treatment that slows the progress of the parasite down now, but no cure and no way to inoculate anyone against it. Meanwhile, good old Niko is out there spreading it just as fast as he can. It's in all the clans now, and the unaligned vamps are dropping like flies. This compound has gone into quarantine, feeding only from the emergency stores. But blood isn't shelf stable. They'll run out soon, and as soon as they start feeding on humans again, this place will be crawling with the infected in no time."

"But the specialized version of the cure worked on me," I said, confused. "Right?"

"In a manner of speaking," Jackson says with a shrug. "We honestly aren't sure. It didn't seem to be working, but . . ."

"But what?" I ask, confused. "If I'm alive, it must have worked."

Jackson rubs the stubble on his chin thoughtfully.

"You feel up to a walk?" he asks.

"Yeah," I say at once, sliding out of bed, only a little wobbly as I stand and grab a robe. "Where are we going?"

He gives me a strange look.

"You wanted to know where Arsen was, right?"

~

Arsen's room is quiet and dark, devoid of the vibrancy of his presence. It feels unnatural, out of context. And Arsen barely looks like himself, pale and thin, his breathing shallow. He doesn't wake when I come to stand beside his bed. Slowly, I sit down beside him, the mattress creaking. I run my hands over the sheets, remembering lying in them together not that long ago.

"He's been out as long as you have," Jackson explains, quietly. "He nearly drained himself dry. Thought he could flush the virus out with a transfusion, I guess. God only knows if it worked. It could have been his blood that saved you. Could have been the cure. Could have been your own antibodies. It was likely some combination of the three."

I nod, understanding. With supplies low and no guarantee the cure that worked for me will work for anyone else, they can't afford to test it. Especially if it possibly requires draining one of their best to the brink of death. Maybe once I can get back to the lab . . .

"Why hasn't he woken up?" I ask, my stomach tying itself in knots. I smooth wrinkles in the sheets like I can do the same to the tangled anxiety within me.

"The lack of blood, I figure." Jackson shrugs. "His people gave him as much as they could spare from the stores, but with the rationing, it was barely enough to keep him alive. Dumbass even made them give the last of the witch blood to you, hoping to strengthen your immunity. And thanks to the virus, we can't get him anything fresh."

He puts a hand on my shoulder, looking a little guilty, and I realize there are tears on my cheeks. I scrub them off quickly, embarrassed.

"He'll pull through," Jackson insists, but his words are uncertain. "He just needs time and blood."

"Then we'd better get to work," I say, clenching my jaw. "The sooner we kill Niko, the sooner everyone can hunt safely."

"Already on it," Jackson replies, with a devilish grin. "I've put the word out to a few other hunters I know. There isn't exactly a community, but everybody knows a few people, who know a few people. And they're all looking for Niko."

"If that show at the Baetal compound was anything to go by, Niko doesn't stand a chance," I say, grinning.

"Well, I wouldn't say that was an average performance for a hunter," Jackson says a little smugly, shrugging. "But yeah, Niko's got a well-deserved reckoning on the way. And once we've got the cure . . ."

He trails off, seeing me staring down at Arsen again. He fidgets with something in his pocket, scratches his chin, retreats to the window, peering through the curtains at the cool, empty night beyond.

"You know," he says, quietly, and I glance up at him, highlighted silver by the moon. "He loves you."

I look away, frowning.

"Or he thinks he does, anyway," Jackson shrugs. "Loves complicated that way. Everybody sees it a little different, and it only really works if you find someone that sees it the same way you do."

"I don't generally include lying and using people in my definition of love," I tell him, remembering Arsen's touch, the way he'd held me. "I wasn't anything to him but a cure. Just something to leverage over everyone else to get himself more power. What is it with vampires and the big stupid political power plays?"

"I know, right?" Jackson scoffs. "It's like a compulsion! Give a guy a couple extra decades of life and suddenly he's Napoleon Fucking Bonaparte."

"Maybe it's a mortality thing?" I ask. "Like, you don't need to eat or worry about money or having kids or a career or anything, which just gives you a ton of free time, and you can only spend so much of that hunting. So you need some dumb drama bullshit to focus on. Like the French aristocracy."

Jackson laughs, brief and harsh.

"All vampires are the French bourgeoisie," he chuckles. "I love it."

Quiet falls between us for a long, still moment. I watch Arsen breath, the steady rise and fall of his chest.

"Claudette warned me, you know," I say, eventually. "That he was a user. I just figured she was bitter. Or projecting."

Jackson frowns at the window. There's something he isn't telling me, which hangs in the air between us, almost tangible.

"It's more complicated than you think," he says, at last. "He fucked up. Don't get me wrong. But sometimes when people are desperate, they do dumb things."

"He lied to me," I say, giving Jackson a hard look. "Maybe he had a good reason, but he didn't trust me enough to tell me what it was. Whatever it is, it's clearly more important to him than me."

Jackson sighs and takes off his hat, leaning against the window frame.

"For what it's worth," he says, "I don't think he wanted to hurt you. Seeing you like that . . . it really hit him."

"So, what?" I ask, tilting my head. "You're on his side now? Big bad vampire hunter?"

"No," Jackson says, quickly. "I still think he's an ass. But he might be a decent ass."

I snort. "I'll make sure to tell him you said that."

"Don't you dare."

"I'm sure he'll be very interested to know that you think his ass is decent."

"Sasha."

I laugh, however briefly, and hang on to a little bit of hope.

Jackson leaves eventually, but I stay, hoping Arsen will wake up. An hour ticks past as I sit near the window, watching him breathe, willing him with every exhalation to open his eyes. A weird, angry impatience rises in me. A kind of desperation that gathers like heat low behind the eyes. Frustration makes me restless. I pick at the arms of the chair. Every second he isn't awake makes the anvil on my heart feel heavier.

"Wake up," I say at last. The moon is getting low outside the window. "Wake. Up."

He doesn't move. I stand up too fast, and the chair falls over. I press down the anger that wants to seize me. When the parasite had me, I learned to be good at that. So I'm calm as I climb over the end of the heavy wooden bedframe and onto the end of the bed.

"There are some things I need to say to you," I tell him, the springs shifting under me. "Important things. Things I'm probably not going to have the guts to say later. So wake up and listen."

But he doesn't, of course. I climb over him, until my hair hangs down like a curtain around us both. He goes on breathing, shallow and weak.

"Get up," I demand. I shake him by the shoulders a little. "Arsen. Get up."

I shake him harder. Still nothing. My eyes sting with tears again. If it weren't for those shallow, barely-there breaths, it would be so easy to think he was truly dead.

"You lied to me," I say, my shoulders shaking. "You used me. I don't care if that's not what you meant. That's how it felt."

I'm crying, my tears falling onto his face. I could almost think it was him crying them as they track down his cheeks. Good. I want him to cry. I want him to feel like I did. If he could cry for me, at least it meant he felt something.

"I was—*am*—was in love with you," I tell him, my hands gripping the sheets in white-knuckled fists to either side of his head. "Or I was starting to be anyway. And you made me feel like I was nothing to you. An object. Do you have any idea how that feels?"

His face is as placid as the moon in sleep, and no number of surrogate tears can change that.

"Do you have any idea," I ask, gripping his shirt, shaking him. "What it's like to love someone who doesn't even see you as a person?! You made me think I could trust you! And then you took it away because you couldn't fucking resist bragging about it to your friends! Wake! Up!"

I slap him. As hard as I'd wanted to slap him when I'd overheard him talking about his ambitions for me. The crack echoes in the empty room. It leaves my hand stinging and a welt on his face, but he doesn't even flinch.

I slip down to lie beside him, feeling stupid, humiliated, and guilty. Who fucking slaps a comatose guy? Even a jerk like Arsen? The kind of asshole who deserves someone like him, probably.

"Then you go and do *this*," I tell him, lying on my side next to him, watching the endless rise and fall of his chest. "What am I supposed to think, Arsen? Wake up. Please, wake up and tell me how I'm supposed to feel. You hurt me. You risked your life for me. You almost died for me. You lied to me."

I stare at him, willing him with every fiber of my being, every beat of my undead heart, to wake up. He doesn't. I curl up against him, my head on his shoulder, and close my eyes.

"What's wrong with me?" I ask him softly, the echoes of the slap still ringing in the corners of the dark room. "Why is it after all of that, I think I still love you?"

He doesn't have an answer, and neither do I. I get up to close the drapes as the sky begins to turn gray with morning, and then I lie down beside him again and close my eyes. The chirping of crickets is replaced with birdsong, but all I hear is his breathing beneath me, and the way it subtly changes as I fall asleep, growing deeper and lower with rest.

CHAPTER 2

I am beside myself.

Arsen lies on his bed, deathly white and frailer than I've ever seen him, trying to heal from his sacrifice. The sacrifice he made to save me. The sacrifice consuming him.

It's not just his handsome blond locks or chiseled face or muscled and ripped body that took such command over me. It was because, despite his utterly ruthless nature when he had a goal to achieve, he was at the same time utterly tender to the people he cared about. All vampires called him a prince, and indeed he was.

Despite his misgivings, Arsen agreed to assign Jackson the role of ambassador to the other vampire clans to inform them of exactly what Niko did. It went against all he believed in, but he did it for the good of vampire kind everywhere—a huge step out of his comfort zone, but he did it because he trusted me.

And he had faith I could come up with a cure when I had failed miserably so many times, I'd opened my heart to him. He trusted me enough to crash into Niko's den and risk his life so that we could find the cure.

Okay. Crazy Demetri had the cure all along. But he received

his reward for that bit of betrayal. The look of surprise on his face when he impaled himself on the stool I held up to defend myself was precious. In a secret part of my emerging vampire heart, it was a luscious moment. If I wasn't half out of it by how sick I was, I would have enjoyed his death more.

I shiver. As a human, I relish no one's death. But I'm not human anymore. I am a predator, and the same gusto Arsen took in defeating me and Niko in the Provokar, I took in watching Demetri die impaled on a stool leg.

How do I live with my bloodthirst? It is difficult.

So far, I've been able to do it by equating donation bags with juice bags, but blood is not juice. At least not fruit juice. It's human juice and raises all sorts of red flags. But now it seems as natural to me as sipping on a juice box. It's sick, I tell you, and natural, and I'm so confused, my head hurts.

The only thing I'm not confused about is Arsen fighting for his life. If I need to, I will offer my own wrist to his fangs if it will help him. But will that help or hurt? Until I run tests on my blood, I can't be sure if the parasite is flushed or hiding in my tissues waiting to emerge to cause more suffering.

Arsen's lips curl at one side and he shivers. I rush to the bed, which barely dips as I sit on the edge and my undead heart stutters as I watch his eyelids flutter.

This is all my fault . . . my crazy, stupid fault. I dragged him into danger by asking him to go with me to Niko's lab and retrieve my research materials after I had run away without a plan to get away from both Demetri and Niko. In hindsight, I could come up with a half dozen ways to sneak that information out, and no one would have had to get hurt.

The strange irony is that only by going back and fighting both Niko and Demetri did I learn that Demetri, despite his lies, had the cure. He hadn't made it, but he had the formula. I'd half-managed in my dilapidated state, to work on it further.

I should have known that Demetri wasn't the idiot he

pretended to be. But I still couldn't figure out his end game. What did he have to gain from all this? Someone must have promised him something big. I can't imagine Claudette had enough to offer him to make him risk his life against all vampire kind. But what do I know about bloodsuckers besides my limited experience as one? The politics of the community swirl about my head like a murder of crows cawing and fussing, seeming nonsense and of great import at the same time.

Nothing of these people are inconsequential and despite having a cure, we have not produced enough for everyone and I've got to continue. on that. But I can't leave Arsen because I would never forgive myself if something happened to him.

It's irrational. The vampire doctor Arsen had on call told me there was nothing I could do for him. Did he, just like a coma patient, know somewhere deep I was next to him?

I reach for his hand, to hold on to some part of him, and tears flow from my eyes.

"Baby," I say. "Don't leave me. I just got you. I can't lose you at the same time."

A groan comes from deep within him, unearthly, like a cry from the grave, and I suck in my own cry of distress. I cannot face this might be the end of the man I love.

The man I love.

It's a brutal admission, even through all the crap.

But then with a jerk of his unnaturally strong hand, he brings my wrist to his mouth. His mouth opens in a strange rictus, and his fangs descend. Is this a last desperate attempt at life or is he awakening? Either way, I allow it because gazing into his face, there is nothing I will refuse him.

Even my life at his death.

Arsen's slice into my flesh is fire and my blood flows easily into his mouth. His throat works automatically to draw the ichor into his body. The slow primal beat of his heart thrums through my body, and it joins with mine in one rhythm.

We are one and suspended in a singular moment in time and I understand now. Arsen was never in physical danger. He gave me a chance to recover before he took back what he had given me.

We aren't sharing thought in what anyone would consider telepathy. However, we are joined in a connection. Heart to heart, soul to soul, more intimate than the sharing of bodies. From this moment on, we would always know what the other is thinking.

And the more he took of me, the more he took me into himself and I see the desire and passion of his heart and mind. He has been searching for so long for someone that shared his deep concern for the fabric of life. The women he knew wanted him, but they didn't want to care, not in the way he did. They wanted sex or status or wealth. He'd happily live a pauper if it meant he had someone by his side who understood him as an individual.

His loneliness is a consuming black hole eating at his soul. He considered himself a creature out of step with his community. But when he met me, he understood he was a vampire ahead of his time.

This is why he loves me. The universe crafted our souls of the same thread, and our joining created a fabric unique and whole.

No wonder he went to illegal lengths to win me in the Provokar. If he had lost me, it would have meant more soul-eating, inescapable years alone . . . torture for an immortal. A living death.

"Oh, Arsen," I breath. My heart beat slows, and I'm dimly aware he's taking too much but warmth spreads through me as large as the immensity of his love for me. He can have anything he wants. There are no barriers between us.

But he jerks my wrist away, ripping more of my skin in his alarm. "No, Sasha," he says. "I didn't go through all this to lose you."

I urge my lover to drink. But he holds my wrist and just licks at the blood, slowly, sensuously, the tip of his tongue making lazy circles that ignite a fire between my legs. I shake, I want him so badly.

Or is it blood loss?

Arsen pulls the comforter away. "Slip under the blanket, sweetheart. I want to feel your skin against mine. Let me hold you."

Shakily I strip off my clothes, aware that I had to spare these precious seconds not touching him, so that I can get more of him.

"That's right, baby," he whispers. "You are gorgeous, so awesome. I need you, Sasha, here, by my side."

Arsen slides to the side, and I lie next to him. He turns to his side and searches my face, wiping away a tendril of my hair from my forehead.

"Are you okay?" he asks, tenderly. "I think I took too much."

"Then give some back," I say, and he smiles. "We'll always share like this." He offers me his wrist, the same one I had drained him before, but it is different this time as I bite down. He gasps, but it is a sound of pleasure. He juts his hip into mine so that the steel of his shaft makes an urgent demand.

Our blood mingles and I taste him and me in the plasma I suck and I expand with wonder at this sharing. Then Arsen pulls away.

"Greedy," he says, but his eyes shine with warmth.

"I'll always want you. For now. Forever."

"Of course," he says with insufferable vampire arrogance, but then he winks to clue me of his teasing.

"So, you better get at," I say, brazenly.

"At what?" he says with innocence.

"Fucking me until I scream your name."

"Is this a contest?" Wickedness seeps through his words and I smile because I arouse his natural competitive nature. "Will you try to resist screaming my name?"

"Yes," I say, seductively. "I want you to fuck me so thoroughly that all I can do is scream it."

"Oh, Sasha," he says. "I will make you regret you said that."

"I hope so."

With a sexy growl, he yanks my arms above my head and settles, his legs spread on either side of me, above me. I see his large cock, hard and weeping precum, pointing straight at me and I try to lift my head so I can lick the tip. Arsen shakes his head.

"Hold on to the headboard," he commands. "Don't you dare take your hands off."

"Is that an order?" I ask, teasingly.

"Your prince commands it."

"I see. So, you must command your women to do the things you want."

"Wench!" He lets out in mock exasperation. "What happened to women doing as they are told?"

"Not this wench," I say, firmly.

"You think?" He rises and turns me so I am face down on the bed. With another yank, he pulls me up to me knees.

"You better be ready. You've been begging for this."

"Sir, I never beg."

"You will be," he says, roughly.

And I think I know what he will do, but I am wrong. Holding my hips so tightly I think he'll leave marks with his hands, he lowers his head and kisses and nibbles the globes of my ass. He is everywhere, and it is delicious and torturous because it is good but not enough and a little whine escapes from my mouth.

"Oh, Arsen. Please."

"Is that begging?"

"No."

"I thought so."

He resumes his sweet torture but this time between my butt cheeks and I jump. I never imagined that area would be so sensitive, but it is. Delectable shivers run through me and my knees grow so shaky I don't know if I can hold myself up on them. Already my face presses against the pillow, and my legs spread wide open and vulnerable to whatever Arsen wants to do.

Arsen gives me an unexpected playful nip on my butt.

"How you doing, there, babe?" he teases, evilly. "Ready to beg yet?"

"Not yet."

"Let me see what I can do about that."

He dips his head lower, and oh dear lord, laves my folds from front to back. I'm clawing the sheets, pressing my mouth into the pillow to keep from screaming out. It's so good I don't want him to stop ever, and the universe could go to hell if Arsen wants to stay between my legs with his tongue.

The evil bastard hits my clit and batters it over and over with loving licks, and I want to scream. I am a mess now, slobbering into the pillow, whole body shaking as jolts of pleasure travel my spine. I'm unsure if I can hold out much longer.

Arsen pulls his head away and sighs.

I think about saying, "No! Don't stop." But I don't because I want to see what new torture the rogue has for me.

"I can see you are incorrigible. I must go to further lengths to get you to beg properly."

"I'd like to see you try," I choke out.

A resounding slap jiggles my butt. What otherwise would be pain transmutes by his previous relentless assault into pleasure, and my core tightens in the delightful burn of imminent orgasm. If he does that again, I will come.

But Arsen doesn't. He enters, hard and rough, and fills me with his cock and nothing ever feels this good. I'm on the edge anyway, but instead of moving, he holds his hard cock inside me and I am wild at being held at the edge of orgasm.

"Tell me you want me," Arsen says.

"I want you," I choke out.

"Tell me you need me."

"Oh dear god, I need you, Arsen."

"Tell me to fuck you. Beg for it, Sasha. Beg for me to fuck you."

I shook my head defiantly.

"I see," he says, coolly.

His cock is hard within me and I feel the blood pulsing through it but he doesn't move, and I want it, him too. I need the push and pull of him inside, the heat of friction within to light that final blaze. But Arsen will not deliver until I say the words he wants from me.

My body burns, my mind stares at the edge of the conflagration that gathers between my legs and spreads through my body in relentless suspension. Never move did I need this—him—so much that I cannot help my next words.

"Please, Arsen. Fuck me. Fuck me hard."

He bent and kissed my neck tenderly.

"Your wish, my lady, is my command."

CHAPTER 3

I wake as if from a fever dream, disoriented and unable to piece together where I am. And flashes of Arsen inside me, outside of me, nibbling every part of my body, biting my shoulder flood my consciousness. If that didn't tell me Arsen fucked me six ways to Sunday then the residual throbbing in my core did. We had overdone it in every way possible and I just passed out from exhaustion.

But my body, from the residual aftershocks, tells me it is looking for rounds two, three and four. Who knew vampires have such stamina? Arsen apparently does because I had woken briefly in the night and found him clutching me, still hard within me. It was a sweet moment that also starkly illustrated the difference between human and vampire men.

No wonder Claudette wants him back. Well, too fucking bad. He is mine now and I don't share. She better stay out of my way or I'll lay her out flatter than a rug just for general principles. This makes me smile way more than it should.

But as I fully wake, I realize a distressing thing. Arsen is not in the bed. What is he up to now? I prop myself on my elbows sweeping the room, checking if he sits at the desk to the right, in one chair by the fireplace on the left, but nope.

Arsen left me alone.

Irrationally, I fear I displease him and that I am not enough for a vampire that had more lovers than rocks in the asteroid field. This is a crazy idea because I felt the bottomless depths of his love last night, and his unstoppable passion.

The door creaks open and surprised, I gather the comforter to my breast and Arsen walked in with a tray of donation bags.

"I brought breakfast." Arsen sits on the bed and holds out the tray to me.

"Hmm, my favorite." Like a gentleman he offers me first pick, and it turns out I choose a very ordinary O positive. But I don't care. I'm not some of these vamps who determine status by the company you drink.

"Where did you go?" I ask.

"Miss me?"

"Yes, you scamp. I did."

"Scamp? I'm that now?"

"Yes," I say with authority.

"I see. Well, first thing I did was tell everyone that you are my mate, and they are to do what you tell them without question."

"Oh, really? One good fuck and I'm Lady of the Manor."

"To be technical about it, it was more than one good fuck."

"Ah, you're right about that. Though I'm fuzzy on the details."

"Good, then I did my job."

"I see. And tell me what does this 'Lady of the Manor' business mean?"

"It means you are to be ready to hop into bed whenever I say."

"Does it now? Are there some sort Lady of the Manor bylaws I should consult? Because that sounds awfully convenient for you."

"How's that?"

"Well, what about when I want to go to bed? Is the Lord of the Manor similarly obligated to occupy the bed?"

Arsen strokes his chin. "I'm not sure because I never had an official Lady of the Manor before."

This bit of information floors me and I stare at him.

"But Claudette—"

"Claudette talks a lot of shit. The truth is she had her affairs and I had mine. It's not my fault that she thought we had more than I offered."

Okey dokey, then.

"She didn't get the memo," I say.

"Don't worry about Claudette. She's my problem. Now drink up. You need your strength."

Hefting the bag in my hand, I slice the pouch with my fangs and suck it in. I am hungry and the bag is empty within a minute. Arsen smiles at me indulgently. "Have another," he urges.

"Not until you have yours."

"Hmm," he says thoughtfully. "Defiant and bossy."

"That's why you love me."

"Oh, I love you?"

"Don't you?"

"Yes. You wench."

"I didn't know I was signing up on a pirate."

He scowls sexily. "Pirate?"

"Your excessive use of the word 'wench.'"

"Other people used the word 'wench.' It was a common enough term during a more uncivilized time."

"Not in this century. Drink up."

Arsen realizes his is beat because he tears into the pouch and drinks while keeping one eye on me.

"Where did you go?" I ask. "Not just to get these. Anyone would have brought these to you."

"You're right. I checked on things,"

"Like what?"

"Niko seems to have disappeared. Left his coven behind."

"That's weird. I wonder why?" It's not like him to retreat. Or leave his beloved powerbase behind.

"Yes, it is very strange. Niko is their prince, but he has abandoned them. I can't figure an advantage in that, and Niko only does what gives him an advantage." Arsen replies.

I raise a brow. "He doesn't care a thing about them, except as extensions of his power."

"I agree he doesn't care, but why did you say the thing about extensions of power?" he asks.

"It's was something he told Demetri when he didn't know I was listening. Each fledgling, because they drank his blood, was a part of him, subject to his directions and therefore increased his sphere of influence."

"That is a common attitude among the princes of the different clans. The Kresova Queen is even worse. She considers all her subjects her slaves. Her favorite ones she calls 'her pets' and she treats them like that."

"She continues to sound horrible." I shudder.

"The worst of the worst. But we still have no explanation for Niko abandoning his coven."

Arsen is right. It makes little sense. Niko is power-hungry and I can't see how leaving behind his followers will help him gain power. He only wants a few to get sick to throw suspicion off himself and from his conversation in the lab with Demetri, fully expects to have most of his coven at his beck and call.

"Did you see your sister while you were 'checking things out'?"

He nods his head.

"How's she doing?"

Arsen shrugs. "About the same. No improvement."

"She didn't get the cure?"

"No one can make it."

"There's Jackson."

"And with me out of it, do you think my people will let him in the door?"

Arsen is right. No sane vampire will let the most feared vampire hunter in the door even if wearing a sign that says, "I'm your next best hope for survival."

"That's too bad. Jackson and I made an agreement. He won't kill any vampires that do no harm to humans."

"Yes. It is a fantastic agreement."

I can't tell if Arsen is being sarcastic or perhaps he means "fantastic" in the more mundane meaning as "unbelievable."

"Just so you know, I changed the orders at the door to allow Jackson in."

I don't expect this and give Arsen a searing kiss. God, I miss my best friend, and I want to know how he came out of the mess at Niko's house. I'll call him in a few and ask him to come over. Besides, I'm going to need his help for what I will do next.

"You are awesome," I say.

I hop out of bed and start the search for my clothes, which found curious places to hide during last night's festivities. T-shirt, jeans, bra, and panties are behind chairs, under the desk, and the bed. Clutching my panties and catching the scent of last night's arousal churns desire in me. We will need to do something about getting more of my clothes here.

"Question. Just for logistics' sake, I am moving in, right?"

"Of course. Where else would you live?"

"I do have an apartment off-campus. I have a lease."

"Don't concern yourself. I'll get my lawyers on it. If need be, I'll just pay the lease."

I kiss his cheek.

"That's what I like about you. Insufferably rich."

"Is that all?" he says, quirking an eyebrow.

"Nope. Your big dick."

He pulls me on top of him, which demonstrates how big said

dick is as it presses into my stomach while he gives me a kiss that sizzles hot enough to curl my toes.

"Mmm," I murmur in appreciation, and then vainly try to pull away. But he's too strong, as usual, and we stare at each other, he with a look of lust that makes me reconsider my plan. But Sasha Keleterina does not get to superstar graduate student status by laying down on the job, no matter how much I want to.

"I've got to go."

"Go? Where? For what?"

"To get to work on mass producing the cure. I've already been too selfish as it is."

"You and I are still recovering from everything, Sasha. I understand if you want to wait a day or two and gather your strength. Nothing will change."

"You're right. If things had been status quo, there is no reason to think they will change drastically. But to get this done, I must get back to the school lab and produce more cure."

"Career women," Arsen huffs. "If you insist on leaving my bed, at least don't go far. In fact, you don't have to."

"What do you mean?"

"I'll show you." He pulls on a pair of pants and throws on a silk bathrobe, fully dressed as the Lord of the Manor instead of a sex-starved stud. I push back my lust as he takes my hand and leads me down the hall.

My sharpened vampire senses catches a faint difference from the scent of the hallway and I wonder what is up. At a door with a fancy security pad, he presses his finger in the center and the door swings open automatically. Arsen sticks his hand inside and the room within lights in fluorescent brilliance.

Holy shit. Arsen has built a lab facility on his compound and it's better than Niko's. In a trance, I walk to the state-of-an-art electron microscope and caress it.

Arsen laughs and it breaks me out of my shock.

"I think you love that thing more than you love me."

"Oh no. Each has its uses. I use this for hard science. You? Hard biology."

He comes up behind me and put his arms around my waist.

"I don't think I mind as much as I should," he says. Arsen plants several nibbles on my neck and hits a spot that is as sensitive as an erogenous zone.

"What's that?" I ask.

"Mmm," he says, licking behind my ear. "My mating bite."

"What?"

"It shouldn't be a surprise. You gave me one, too."

"I may have given you a hickey or two."

"No, Sasha," he rumbles in my ear. The sound shoots straight between my legs. "You do not give hickeys with your fangs."

"I sunk my fangs into your neck?"

"My, my," he says with a voice that is too self-satisfied. "Don't remember? Did I fuck your brains out, too?"

"I remember you torturing me with pleasure until I begged for you. After that the details are hazy."

"And you love it, wench."

Arsen pulls me tightly against his hips and again he's as hard as a rock. He grinds against my ass.

"You should return to bed. As you see you have everything you need to pursue whatever work you want to do here whenever you want to. There is no need to expose yourself needlessly to the dangers of human exposure."

"I can't believe that you built this for me."

"I didn't."

"Oh?"

"What Niko did made me realize how vulnerable we all are to the advances of human science. They no longer need wooden stakes or take dangerous chances to eradicate us. And we need to keep our work secret, otherwise humans will find other ways to exploit us. Sasha, I need you for me. But my people need you for the skills you have."

For the briefest glimmer of time, I remember what Claudette said about Arsen using people until he had no more need of them. But I have shared . . . do share a part of Arsen's soul and I can't believe he would cast me aside. This might make me the biggest vampire fool on this side of the Atlantic. I look over my shoulder and into his eyes and I see a man whose eyes shine with love. Will they shine like that for me forever? I don't know. All we have is now, and I take now.

But I still have reservations.

"That's a lot of responsibility. I haven't even finished my studies yet."

"You will. Whatever it takes, whatever resources you need, you'll get it. You're my consort now, part of the Draugur, and what's mine is yours."

"Aren't you afraid of what kind of divorce settlement that will mean?"

"Who says I'd allow a divorce, wench?" He nips the skin at the base of my skull. I curse because the pain and pleasure mix sweetly and I want to spread my legs and take him right here, which might be what he intends all along.

"Allow, allow," I complain as he sucks on my spine and makes me grip the steel lab table with my hands. "You're so bossy."

"That's my job. Boss around the wenches and make sure the important works gets done."

"Well, you're failing at that because you make me want to play, not work."

"That is also my job."

"So, you can't lose, can you?"

"I never do, Sasha," he says.

He reaches his hand around and strokes my mound through my jeans, and I throw my head back onto his shoulder.

"I'm going to lose my sterile field if you keep that up."

"Whatever that is, I'll pay to fix it." He reaches farther and draws his fingers up in one long continuous slide that makes me stand on tiptoe.

"You're impossible," I gasp. My pants soak once again with my cream and all I can do is squirm on Arsen's insistent fingers. I want him now, again and again in any way he will have me.

And then another familiar scent hits my nose and he clears his throat.

"Um . . .huh," says Jackson as he clears his throat. "Hope I'm not interrupting anything."

"Jackson!" I say. I twist away from Arsen and throw my arms around his neck.

"How are you? You worried me! I toss a glance over my shoulder to gauge Arsen's reaction because he has responded poorly to Jackson's presence in the past. But he stands there calmly, without a flicker of jealously or territoriality lighting his model handsome face. Well, that's new, but I'll take it as a measure of our cemented relationship.

"I'm fine," says Jackson. "I came to check on you. In fact, I have every day for two weeks. But today was the first day they let me in."

"Sorry about that," says Arsen. "I rectified that when I came to."

"Look. Arsen built me a state-of-the-art lab."

Jackson's jaw twitches as if he isn't fully on board with the lab thing, or it is a memory of the horrific events that took place in Niko's lab.

"That's great, Sasha."

"And you can help me with the next project."

"That's my thought, too, and more than just me, too."

"What do you mean?"

"I'll tell you later. But right now, I need to bring you up to speed on what's going on with the vamps. There is some serious shit going down."

CHAPTER 4

The odor of alcohol clings to everything in the lab.

Clinically, I'm impressed with the simplicity of Demetri's cure. He intended to mass produce this at the lowest cost while selling it to desperate vampires for an insane amount of money. Someone had to fund his research to create this thing, generated from the most innocuous of viruses turned deadly with few biomechanical tweaks. Now that I know what to look for, I feel stupid for not picking up on it sooner.

That bastard Demetri chose the West Nile virus to play mad scientist with, though I suspect he got his ideas from dengue fever. Both viruses adhere to red blood cells, though dengue does it more lethally. But because of its deadly potential, the samples are locked up more securely than a Mafia don in federal prison. West Nile also likes to seep through the brain/blood barrier of the brain and infect brain cells, making it nearly as dangerous as meningitis. The modifications that Demetri made turned the thing into a moderately dangerous virus to a lethal one, exploding blood and brain cells as fast as it could reproduce.

No wonder vampires went mad. The pain alone would be excruciating.

And me?

Well, I had to dig deep into my brain for that one, but I dimly remember when I was five that I got very sick. Now, looking at my old blood samples Jackson had retrieved from Niko's lab and knowing what to look for, I found the antibodies for West Nile virus. And the same antibodies interfered with the parasite just at a slower rate, so those fuckers were already on the road to purgatory before Arsen made me feed from him. It might be Arsen's sacrifice wasn't necessary, but I won't tell him. Our shared blood binds us, which is the best thing to happen out of this entire mess.

So I have a couple answers and a lot of antiviral to make up and I am not a factory. I could really use Jackson's help that he promised more in the cryptic way, but right now I'm going it alone.

My bra buzzes and I'm so deep into my work, my brain doesn't connect with where my phone is. I pull it out to see Niko's ugly mug beneath his number.

Screw him. I put the phone done and continue my work.

It rings again, and I push the button to make it go to voicemail. Then I turn it off, which gives me a few more uninterrupted minutes.

I hear another ring deeper toward the back of the room and I realize it is the lab landline Arsen has installed. Damn it. I'll never get any work done. But I answer. It is probably an impatient Arsen because I told him I would call when I had another batch done, so we could administer a dose to his sister.

"Sasha," says Niko

What the fucking hell! Who let this call come in? When I find out there might be a beheading involved.

"I'm hanging up, Niko. Don't bother calling me again, or I'll find you and separate your head from its body myself."

He laughs. "You always are good with the jokes. How's

bedding Arsen? Everything you'd dream it would be or are you ready for a real man?"

I scoff loudly to drive home the point.

"That's childish even for you."

In the background I hear a public address system, though I don't make out the exact words.

"Sasha, I don't have a lot of time here, but I'm giving you one more chance to come with me. I'm your maker and you owe me your allegiance. There is a place beside me for you."

"I owe you nothing," I say.

"Arsen doesn't recognize your value, what you can become. Under him you'll remain little Sasha, starry-eyed sycophant for the man who would be king but doesn't have the balls to do it."

"You know what I don't have, Niko? Patience for you. Don't call me again."

Slamming the headset into the cradle feels good until the phone breaks in half. I'm not used to my vampire strength which has grown since Arsen cured me of my different illnesses. Hopefully, Arsen won't be too angry with me.

The door to the lab swings open and it can be only one of two people that have access to the lab, Arsen or Jackson. I will be glad to see either one.

"Hey, babe," says Arsen. "How's the work coming along?"

"Well, I'm nearly done with this batch. We'll be ready to take it to your sister in just a few minutes."

"Good. I'm thinking you are working too hard and we should take a break."

"A bedroom break? Or are you going to take me on an actual date?"

"Date? What is that?" Arsen has mischief in his eyes when he wants to tease me, and I see it now. There are times when he deliberately ignores the modern word for what I'm trying to say, though he damn well knows it.

"I believe you may have called it courting."

"Is that when you are trying to get a woman into your bed? I'm seem to recall you being there already."

"Hey, it's the twenty-first century. If a man doesn't put out, he might find himself alone in the bed."

"Uh huh," he says with a smile, and he wraps his arms around me. "Don't try to run. I'm faster than you, and I'll catch you."

"The Provokar proved who was faster."

"Naw, I let you run ahead. I had too much fun throwing fireballs. Don't get too much of a chance to toss those."

Arsen lowers his mouth to capture mine in a kiss, and it feels so good, I don't want him to stop. But the timer rings signaling the batch is done, and I need to pull it out before it's ruined.

"Excuse me. Mission of Mercy takes precedence over making out."

"Says who?"

"Says Dr. Sasha, Medicine Woman. Step aside, kind sir, and let me amaze you."

"I'm already amazed at how you can resist me."

"It's tough," I say, throwing my forearm across my head dramatically. "But sacrifices must be made to science."

I take my batch out of the centrifuge and cap the vials and put them in a rack.

"How do you like my home cooking?"

"Not as tasty as you, Sasha."

"Work first. Dinner later."

"Is that a date?"

"Oh? You're familiar with what a date is now?"

"No, you assumed I didn't know what a date was. But I intend to prove otherwise."

"Bring it, big boy. I want to see what you got."

"It's not a question of what I've got. It's what you can take."

"Oooh, big words."

"And you have a big mouth. Which I will put to use later, since you are hell bent on working."

"Bent?" I say.

"Yeah, you want me to bend you over. I'll do that, too."

"I'm taking that as a promise."

"Take it any way you want to, babe. I'll give it to you anyway you want."

I wonder if this is gallows humor on Arsen's part. That he's joking to shore himself up for the task ahead. Arsen seems reluctant to take this step and hasn't been in a hurry to administer the cure to his sister, Annabelle. He doesn't talk about her condition, either. The last time I saw her she was nearly feral and tried to attack me despite her restraints. I've been too busy to see Arsen's sister, and he didn't exactly encourage me to do so. Maybe she is further gone than he lets on and doesn't want to let her go, even if that's the best thing for her.

I pull some syringes from the supply closet and take a couple vials.

"Let's get this done."

Arsen's demeanor changes as soon as we leave the lab. We walk to his sister's room. We enter, and Claudette slinks away. She glares at me through narrowed eyes, and if she could she'd make her own Provokar on me. But Arsen and I have mated. He has declared it through the coven, and there is nothing she can do other than wish for my death.

Or plot it. One never knows with Claudette.

Arsen's sister's arms are lashed to the bed, but she lays limply as if all the fight has gone from her.

"Arsen? You said she was the same."

"She's been like this for a couple weeks."

"There's a chance this could hurt her rather than cure her, especially in a weakened state."

Arsen closes his eyes and sighs. "We have to try."

I nod and fill a syringe.

"Hold her arm."

Arsen's sister stares upward at the ceiling, and her lip

trembles but she does not cry out or try to thrash like the last time I was here. I swallow hard, staring at her limp form and feminine face so much like Arsen's. What would it do to Arsen if she died? He seems resigned to the possibly but as I learned in my Psychology of Death class, people can seem prepared, but fall apart when it happens. What would it mean for all of us if Arsen fell apart? Who would lead the Draugur? What would I do if faced with an inconsolable vampire with a burning need for revenge?

I work to still my hands so they don't shake as I put the needle to her skin. I find a thin vein and pray it won't collapse. Arsen's sister whimpers but otherwise doesn't move and I pump the medicine into her. If it works as well on her as me, this will cure her.

If not, it means her death.

I pull the syringe out and snap the sharp end off and toss them both into a baggie I'll dispose of in the lab.

"That's all I can do," I say.

"This is," says Arsen as he held his sister's hand, "more than anyone has done. I haven't told you—all the risks you took. What you've been through. I'm very grateful, Sasha. Someone like you, who does the right thing because it's the right thing, that's very rare in my—our world."

"You give me too much credit," I say. "I've just been trying to survive and to make sense of all of this."

"And I'm so proud of you for how you've come through all this. Even if my sister doesn't survive this, I'll still be grateful. And now I must ask more of you. Tomorrow, I need you to sit with me at a conference and talk with some vampires about what Niko did."

"What's going on?"

"I've done my best to convince them, but there are some that do not believe that a human sickness can affect a vampire. And we've had centuries of walking among humans, taking them in all states of health, and not a single vampire got ill from drinking a sick donor. They think we are immune. You must tell them the thing that Demetri did. We must convince them to help capture and put away Niko."

"If you can't, how can I?"

"You can tell them how Demetri made the virus. They aren't uneducated, just unconvinced."

I remember how well Niko did during my quiz during the Provokar and how impressed I was that he answered many science questions correctly. Those librarian vampires must do more than shelve old books. I vastly underestimated the amount of knowledge a vampire can gain over the centuries.

"One vampire lord will listen. He's a friend and owes me a favor. The others think they are above me and don't need to listen. Between my friend and you, we may be able to get the others to come around."

"Arsen, I hate to break your bubble, but is it possible, considering the paranoid nature of vampires, that they'll think it's you that started the virus? That your new consort, the one with the convenient education in rare bloods, may be the one that crafted this illness?"

"That's possible. But I will be there to protect you."

I shiver because once again Arsen conveniently downplays the danger to myself and him in engaging other vampires. I've seen the level of animus between Arsen and Niko, and one is not safe in the same room with them. I have the bruises to prove it until they heal. Now, new vampires on Arsen's property? Ones that don't regard him well? And these guys rarely travel anywhere alone. The idea jacks my nerves to a new height.

"It's important that we get the other vampires together on this. Niko is a danger. Now that he bought one scientist to do his bidding, he'll buy others. He's power-hungry, and he wants nothing more than the murder of all Draugur and possibly the other covens."

"I'll do what I can."

"That's what Jackson said."

Surprise wings through me. "You talked with Jackson?"

"Yes, we've been working together. Jackson is reaching out to his contacts too, to help locate Niko."

"I didn't know you were working so hard to find him. Niko called me today."

"Why didn't you tell me?"

"Honestly, I thought he was just harassing me. He told me 'there's a place by his side' and a bunch of nonsense. I told him to shove it."

Arsen smiles wryly. "That's my girl. But did he give you any idea where he was?"

"No. But I heard a public address system, like he was at an airport or something."

"When he calls you again, see if you can find out where he is."

"Why would he call?"

"Because he can't stand me having something or rather someone he wants."

Arsen's sister whimpers and I don't know if we are disturbing her.

"Maybe we shouldn't talk about this in front of her. Some scientists think that even when they appear comatose, patients hear everything."

"Good," says Arsen. He drops to his knees by the bed and bends his head as if in prayer and it shocks me. I suppose I shouldn't be. I know very little about Arsen's life before he became a vampire.

"Sweetheart," he says taking her hand. "My little bird, don't leave. Stay. Get well. Sasha made medicine for you. It will make you better. I want you to meet her. She's a wonderful woman. You'll love her as much as I do."

I'm going to cry. Vampires aren't monsters who don't care about anyone. That's not true. Arsen loves his sister, and the depths of it rolls over me. I get no vibes from his sister, and it's clear that she's checked out.

Did we get to her too late? Will she recover?

I touch Arsen's shoulder and he grabs my hand. And we stay there for a long while before he stands and reluctantly walks away.

CHAPTER 5

We start for the staircase that will bring us to Arsen's room, when one of his security men, among other things, answers the door and runs up to him.

"My lord," he said. "We have a representative from the Baetal at the door."

"Bring him to my office," says Arsen. He put his arm around me. "Come. We will talk to this Baetal together."

"You want me there?"

"Whatever this is about involves you. Yes."

We enter to see a Baetal standing by a bookcase with a sour expression on his face. And I recognize him. It's Brady, the vamp I partied with.

"Hi, Brady."

He bows formally, as if he learned how in an ancient court, and he probably did. It is a little at odds with his black turtleneck and slacks. But one thing I've noticed is that vampires are usually a strange mix of old-fashioned gentility and ruthless murderer.

"My Lady Draugur, Lord Draugur, I am pleased the lady is well."

"No thanks to the Baetal that attacked me."

"Unfortunate," says Brady, puckering his lips in disapproval. "Lord Nicholas ordered the attack. We could not refuse."

"So, Brady," Arsen says slowly, "why are you here?"

"I understand that you have a cure for the virus. My brother is sick. Whatever you want, whatever is in my power to give, my service, my blood, my life even, it is yours, if you help him."

The man stands stock-still, a testament to vampire stoicism. But worry lines crawl from the corner of his eyes. If he knows he truth, of who allowed the virus to infect the Baetal, would he hate Niko? Would he turn his allegiance to Arsen and serve him? Or would he be a spy, a snake in the grass, ready to strike at the first opportune moment?

I glance at Arsen's face and his expression is unreadable.

"Despite," says Arsen, "the ill feelings I hold toward Nicholas, I've never harbored ill will toward the Baetal. I had hoped that Nikolai would uphold the peace he swore to in Brackloon Woods."

"I was there, my lord."

"Good. Then just know that I do this to uphold that peace and honor the promise I made to my father to do so. We will help what Baetal needs it, within the limits of our abilities. Sasha has made a limited quantity of the cure, but there is not enough for all."

"My lord, that is most generous."

"Go. Tell your people we are coming to the compound later tonight. We have other business before then. And if a single one dares to lift a hand to me, Sasha, or whoever is with us, I will kill you without mercy. Do you understand?"

"Of course, my lord. Considering the circumstances, it is more than fair."

"My security will see you out. Be prepared to welcome us. I will not tolerate bad behavior."

"Yes, Lord Draugur."

Brady, escorted by the man who brought him in, leaves us. Arsen stands before the gas fireplace and stares at the flames.

"Are you up for this, Sasha?" he asks without looking at me. "To walk into the Baetal compound again?"

I don't know. The last time I was there I almost died. Niko's mansion holds bad memories. Still, our help will extend an olive branch to the Baetal and we could have another ally in our camp to hunt down Nikolai.

"I'll do what I need to."

"Good." But he still stares pensively into the fire, and I get that something is bothering him.

I slip my arm around his waist and rest my head on his chest. "What's wrong, baby?"

He shakes his head and draws his lips tight, and this, out of all the shit that's gone down, is the most upset I've seen him.

"I'm worried the other covens will not cooperate and resist our help."

"They've got too," I say stubbornly. "If he could, he'd wipe out all the vampires."

"At least the Draugur. It's always been a Baetal goal, though my father and I thought cooler heads prevailed recently."

"Your father? You've never mentioned him before today."

"He rules over sections of Europe. He sent me here a while ago to set up holdings in the New World."

"Wait? New World. Like in the original colonies?"

"Yes. I was only, let's see, two hundred and fifty years old then. Competition was fierce with the Baetal, Istria, and Kresova, all who had the same idea. I started with a tobacco plantation, which was very lucrative, but the Civil War destroyed it. We pushed west when I heard about gold in the Rocky Mountains a couple hundred years later. The coven pulled a lot of gold out of the hills until the veins ran dry. The money I made thrilled my father. I bought real estate after with cash, so we weathered the Depression just fine. We herded cattle while I waited for the price of land to rebound. Then after the Second World War and the housing boom, I sold a lot of land. This created another fortune, though now I wish I had hung onto more of the land.

"The point of all this is unlike the other covens, we just took care of business instead of fighting it out with the Istria, Baetal and Kresova. And that made me look weak to the other covens. I'm supposed to step into the master position when my father retires. I suspect my father keeps those plans on hold until I establish my authority in North America.

"And I haven't done that well. My sister is sick—"

"But that's not your fault."

Arsen purses his lips and looks away. "That's not the point. I wasn't able to protect her and a Master's job is to protect his coven. She didn't have to join my coven. She could have stayed with our father. But she came with me, trusted me enough to protect her like I should."

"Arsen," I sigh. "Women do not need protection. Not like that."

"Sasha," Arsen says sadly, "have you not learned that we are a people out of time? Civilizations rise around us, humanity changes and evolves, but we also have witnessed how easily humans destroy themselves if one of their changes proves ill. We adopt things from the outside world slowly. Otherwise with our fewer number we'd get wiped out."

"Well, Niko didn't seem to adopt things slowly. And just where did he get his scientific knowledge anyway? I mean he did quite well in the Provokar."

"Niko? During the Age of Enlightenment, he worked with those who developed the scientific method. He was a very young vampire, and it was a scandal for him with his father and coven. But science never stopped fascinating him even when he had to step back because it was apparent that he did not age."

This stops me in my tracks. I only thought vampires were concerned about feeding and status games, not contributing to the development of science. This thing between Arsen and Niko is a very, very old rivalry. At that moment I feel very young and very foolish. But I also realize I underestimated Niko's danger.

Here is a guy who worked with the foundations of science as we know it. He presumably understands the importance that whatever knowledge humans gain, it's for the betterment, not the destruction of mankind or vampire kind. It's a bedrock idea at the foundation of all we do as scientists. And Niko just doesn't care. He has no qualms about perverting the aims of science for whatever single-minded goal he has. Niko is a monster, not because he is a vampire but because he is a sociopath.

"Wow, Arsen. Just wow."

He gazes at me. "Have I blown your mind?"

"In all ways, babe," I say, as an attempt at humor. But it falls flat and Arsen doesn't smile. "I mean, it's your ruthlessness or lack of it that marks your strength as a leader, right?"

"It's always been that way for us. But you did not help."

"Me? What did I have to do with it?" I ask.

"I won you in the Provokar and you ran away."

"You did not win me. You cheated."

Arsen rubs his jaw with one hand. "Points of law aside, what it looked like is that you had no respect for me and ran back to the maker who lost. You made the weaker vampire look like the stronger one."

I bite my lip. I may not agree with what he says, but I see his point.

"And on top of it, I'm working with your friend Jackson, a vampire hunter that is, as you would say, a rock star of vampire hunters."

If this conversation isn't so serious, I would giggle. But again, I feel like an idiot because all these years I had not a single clue what Jackson did on the nights he blew off a study date. Or took the time to find out what he did on those long weekends, supposedly at family outings. But maybe my nerdy self just was so glad to have a friend I didn't look so closely at the times

Jackson and I didn't hang out. And now Jackson Is a rock star vampire hunter?

So Arsen blows my mind once again.

"So you see, my love, to the other covens I've just plain lost my mind."

Oh shit. This is my fault. I made him appear weak after leaving him after the Provokar. I insisted he work with Jackson. Me, in my big brain nerd pride thought I knew what was best for everyone. And Arsen, because he trusted me, went along.

When I'm going to learn not to listen to my big brain?

A knock at the office door rolls through the room.

"Yes," says Arsen loudly.

"My lord, Sir Mallory is at the door along with representatives of the Istria."

"No Kresova?"

"No, my lord."

"And the vampire hunter?"

"Here, with some friends," hisses the vamp in disapproval. "We searched them to make sure they have no weapons."

"Escort them to the dining room," Arsen says. The security man shuts the door.

Arsen sighs. "Without the Kresova . . . They are the strongest of us in the New World."

"Arsen, if the Kresova doesn't want to join the party, that's on them."

He shrugs but he is unhappy about the situation. I squeeze his hand as we walk into the dining room where a long mahogany stretches the length of it. A gorgeous oriental rug lies on the stone tiles, and heavy drapes hang on the windows. A fireplace is in the center of the outside wall, and a gas fire dances within. But even with the magnificent surroundings, the atmosphere, electric with tension, makes me want to flee. On the fireplace side stands a group of eight vampires, and on the other side, Jackson and some humans I haven't met before. They stare at each other, each side waiting for the other to make the first move. At the door stands six of Arsen's security, dressed in black, eyes hidden by sunglasses. They hold their hands clasped before them with their legs spread, at the ready to quell any problems. Their jaws are tight, and it doesn't take basic math to figure they are not happy with this meeting.

"Ah, Arsen," says one vampire with a smile. He stands taller than Arsen, but thinner and his hair hangs in a golden cascade past his shoulders. What I would give to find out what hair products he uses.

"Mallory," says Arsen warmly. Mallory steps forward and clasps Arsen's shoulder. "It's good to see you."

"Same here."

"And this must be your lady, the one we've heard so much about."

"Sasha Keleterina, Lord Mallory Nash of the Baetal. He's second to Nikolai."

"We'll see for how long," says Mallory, with a charming smile. Why do I get the impression he is a rattler waiting to strike?

"At your service," says Mallory, lifting my outstretched hand and kissing it. Is it my imagination or does Arsen's jaw tighten?

"And the man at the fireplace in the center is Lord Gheorghe Agaricu of the Istria."

"Nice to meet you," I say.

The Istria lord raises an eyebrow as if my greeting is graceless and garish. And I suppose in this room chock full of old-world manners it is.

"The pleasure is mine," he says dryly.

"Good. Shall we get to business? Please sit, friends. Henri, have the refreshments brought in," Arsen says.

I shivered because I do not know what refreshments means, and I remember the conversations at the Provokar of different ways to serve up humans.

But a servant brings several decanters of blood. I sniff its scent right away. She pours a glass for Arsen, who raises it and drinks. The woman serves the others.

I sit kitty-corner to Arsen at the head of the table and he pushes his knee into mine.

"Drink," he whispers. "Otherwise, they'll think I poisoned it."

I resist an eye roll and drink the blood, which is tasty. I've moved past tolerating blood for sustenance to appreciating it. I'm shedding humanity faster than I had expected. I glances at Jackson, sitting at the other end, who eyes the glass with distaste.

"So, Arsen," says Gheorghe, rolling the glass stem between his fingers, "we've heard this story from your emissary here, how Nikolai Jederick commissioned a virus to destroy vampires. The question is why should we trust you?"

"Arsen's telling the truth," blurts out Jackson. Gheorghe stares at him like Jackson is a bug to squash.

"It is not my place to dictate who my host allows as guests," snaps Gheorghe, "but at any table the inferiors do not interrupt the masters when they speak."

Jackson opens his mouth to speak, but Arsen shakes his head and stares at Gheorghe.

"You are correct that guests do not dictate what happens at my table, and at my table, Jackson speaks as the lord for human interests. Are we clear, Gheorghe?"

Mallory's eyes glitter with appreciation at Arsen taking control of this meeting when the Istria lord so clearly wants to.

"Yes, Lord Eskandar," snipes Gheorghe.

"Good. Let's proceed."

"But first," says Mallory. "I'd like to ask Lady Keleterina's permission to speak for the Baetal."

Arsen's jaw sticks out and his eyes narrow. I see once again I'm in the middle of shit for which I did not get the memo.

CHAPTER 6

Holy shit. What is happening now? Has Arsen held something back, once again? We will have a very long talk about this later.

"I'm sure that will be fine," Arsen answers quickly.

"No. I want to hear from Lady Keleterina's mouth."

"I don't understand," I say stupidly.

"Ah," says Gheorghe. "Of course, Lord Eskandar has not had the time to fill you in on all the details. Three things," he says holding up his fingers. "One. You drank Lord Nikolai's blood making you Baetal. Two. You're officially Niko's mate since the Elders rendered results of the Provokar invalid. Three, Lord Nikolai is missing in action. These three things render you are the defacto head of the Baetal in this territory."

Oh holy fuck. I want to look toward Arsen to get his reaction but I dare not. This is a classic dick measuring contest, and both Mallory and Gheorghe look to whittle Arsen down an inch or two. And I will not let that happen. I have to wield some chutzpah of my own.

One dick coming up.

"I'm aware," I say rendering as much hauteur in my voice as possible. "I meant that I assumed Lord Mallory would speak for the Baetal because Arsen invited him, with my approval. Go ahead," I say waving my hand. "Represent away."

But holy fuck. Claudette's words about Arsen loving someone while he had a use for them haunts me once again. Does this mean that through me Arsen hopes to control the Baetal? I see Arsen's offer to help the Baetal in a new light.

"Fine," says Gheorghe. "It makes no difference to me who stands in the place of this whore."

Now I have more than dick to show. Pure rage pours through me and I launch across the table and grab the throat of Gheorghe in one hand and squeeze. He rises from his seat and our eyes lock. Blood trickles from where my nails dig into his neck.

"You are impolite," I say. "And I thought you were such a genteel man. Isn't politeness and protocol a thing with vampires? I might be new but at least I caught that in orientation. Now sit down, shut up, and don't speak until Arsen or me speaks to you."

One vampire in the room gasps and others murmur but I don't pay attention as I bore my will down on his and compel him to sit.

But unlike humans, this is no weak-willed creature unaware of what I did. Our eyes lock and we strive for dominion. A part of me wants to give up, but I figure it is Gheorghe playing with my mind to win this contest.

But Sasha Keleterina does not give up. All I have to do is remember that he called me a whore to call up an extra blast of rage. The bastard falls to his seat gasping as he bats my hand away.

The other vampires and Jackson and his confederates all stare at me in shock. I scoot off the table and look to Arsen whose eyes widen only slightly. But he smiles at me with approval.

The Istria lord opens his mouth, and I cock my head. "Did you forget what I just said?"

He shakes his head.

"Then let's get this show on the road. I have a mission of

mercy to perform, and I suspect that will be a hell of a lot more interesting than measuring my imaginary dick to yours."

Arsen fills them in on Niko's activities, and how many of the Draugur are affected. The Baetal lord, when queried, gives us his number of infected and where. Arsen pulls out his phone and maps it.

"It's going across country," I say.

"Yes," says Jackson grimly, "and since the virus can linger six months before it manifests, Niko put the virus out to infect the other vampires at least that long ago."

"How do you know this?" demands Mallory.

"Because I've been helping Sasha with her research."

The other vampires explode, some in exclamations. But it is an Istria sitting next to Gheorghe that says, "How do we know it wasn't Lady Keleterina who made this thing?"

"Sasha didn't even meet Nikolai until a month ago," says Jackson. "And point of fact, he turned her to get back at me because we've been friends since our teen years. The coward wouldn't attack me, so he picked on Sasha."

I cross my arms. "You are welcome to review all my dated work in my notebooks. And if you still don't believe me, then that's just fine. The fact is, I and Arsen control the cure, and if you want it, you'll help find Niko. Because if we don't, then he'll keep implementing his crazy plan. And if you don't, then you'll die. And I tell you that's a better deal than Niko would offer you. He'd bleed you dry financially so you could save your lives."

"That does sound like Nikolai," agrees Mallory. "I will talk with the other Baetal lords. He has many holdings throughout the United States, and he will have to show up at one of them."

"You may speak," I say to Gheorghe.

"I will contact my subject lords and see if they have any information on Niko's whereabouts."

"But what if we can't find Nikolai?" says Mallory. "He's slippery and difficult to track."

"We'll find him," I say with more confidence than I feel. "We have more than one source of information." I get up to leave and I wave Jackson to join me. He and his vampire hunter friends follow, probably relieved to be out of that room of bloodsuckers.

"I'll see you out," I say.

"Wow," says Jackson. "I didn't know you were so badassed."

"Yeah, desperate times and all that." I stop in the hallway and face the vampire hunters who all, except Jackson, glare at me.

"Whatever contacts you have, we need the same information from you. Rates of infection, location, and any Niko sightings."

"We should let you all die," mutters one in the back.

"And as I pointed out to Jackson, before that happened, a whole lot of humans would suffer, so no. Your best bet is in controlling, not eradicating the vampire population. Because from what I can see, there is an entire world of vampires out there who'd love fresh hunting grounds. So far, this virus is confined to North America. Better the devil you know. I have it on good authority that should the Kresova Queen show up, you'd be in big shit. Let's not start another chorus of 'Let the Vampires Die' song. It's boring and has no beat."

My joke floats like a lead balloon.

"Don't worry, Sasha. I wanted them to see for themselves what's at stake."

"Is that a bad vampire hunter joke?"

"Yes," he says with a smile. "We'll get what info we can."

The other vampires in the coven watch from the shadows as the vampire hunters leave. As the door shuts, they hiss and mutter curses.

"Hey," I say, filled with my new authority. "Do you not have something else to do besides eavesdrop on my guests? If you do, do it. If you don't, I've got work for you."

The whispers of footsteps and rattling of doors follow my words. There is nothing like the promise of work to clear a hall. I go to the lab and work on more batches of the cure until Arsen comes to the lab. And I almost dread this because of the conversation we must have.

He walks behind me and puts his arms around me and kisses my neck.

"You were magnificent," he murmurs.

"Thanks," I say dryly. "Just fulfilling my role as leader of the Baetal coven."

Arsen stiffens behind me and I turn to face him, which is a little uncomfortable since he is so close. I bend backward toward the table.

"Why didn't you tell me?" My eyes are narrowed because I'm working up a good mad.

"I didn't want you to think—"

"What? That you wanted me for my position, not for me?"

"Well, yes."

"Idiot," I say.

He steps back as if I struck him.

"I know why you want me, Arsen. We shared blood, remembered." And another thought goes through me. "Wait! We shared blood and I shared Niko's blood. Does that automatically confer some ownership rights to the Baetal to you as my mate?"

If it is possible for a vampire to turn paler, Arsen does at this moment.

"It's not what it sounds like."

"Damn it, Arsen. Is there not a single thing you do that doesn't have a double purpose?"

He closes his eyes.

"It's not like that at all."

"Says you. Can't you be straight for me one time?"

"And how would I explain that to you? Vampire laws are complex."

"And I'm not the smartest person in the room?"

Arsen casts his gaze to the floor and is silent. Then his

sparkling blue eyes blazes and bears into mine. He grabs my wrist and holds it like a vise.

"There are some things smarts or book learning can't help you with. Understanding what it means to be a vampire is not something you can get from a book. It takes a long time. Some never get it before another vampire dispatches them. It means for as long as you live there will be another vampire who will seek your life and take your place. And when you are a prince, like I am, that makes for a very long list of people who want to off you. Anything anyone of us can do to secure and cement our place? We have to do it. That Niko gave you his blood, you are as powerful as you are as a fledgling, and you hold in your head and hands the power to cure our people. How can I not align with you? Sasha, if you don't realize you are my queen, then as smart as you are, you are fool."

I stand and stare at him, flattered and insulted at the same time. There are so many edges to this man—fearsome vampire, devoted leader, passionate lover—they glitter as sharp and bright as diamonds. A light burns in his eyes that tells me he is as consumed with me as I am with him.

I lean my head into his chest and stand. I listen to his heart and realize it beats for me.

"I'm not a fool, Arsen Eskandar."

He straightens. "Good. Then pack your things. I want to get this thing done with the Baetal quickly. I have a queen I want to pay court to."

"Ah, that courting thing again."

"Damn straight."

After all those words, the ride to the Baetal compound is quiet. We keep our own thoughts and Arsen even drives like a sane person, which surprises me.

Arsen pulls the car up to the middle of the driveway that curves in a circle close the door. I turn to pull my supply bag from the back seat when I see a flash of blond hair scurrying away down the long driveway. She is running, which is odd, and from the back it looks like Claudette.

"Who's that?" I say, pointing down the driveway.

Arsen glances in that direction. "Who? What?"

"It looked like Claudette."

"Claudette wouldn't be caught dead in a Baetal compound. Besides, she's attending my sister."

I do not understand Arsen continually defending this woman, but I scan the driveway again and the woman is gone. Only a vampire moves that quickly. But what the hell would Claudette be doing here?

As if they all got the memo to be good little vampires, there is no drama when we arrive. Brady leads me to a room where his brother and several Baetal lie tied to their beds, and my mind flashes to Arsen's sister, lying near comatose on hers. I haven't checked on her, and I should have, though Arsen instructed Claudette to inform him of any change, so I had to assume there isn't one.

But what if she wakes and no one is with her because Claudette is catting around?

This isn't a question I can answer, not now. Arsen murmurs something in my ear about checking some things out while I work. He leaves me alone with the Baetal, my subjects apparently. A couple have only just started showing signs of infection and haven't reached the stage for confinement.

"You can untie them," I say to Brady.

Brady's brother, Nathan, is different story. He is much like Arsen's sister a couple weeks ago, flailing, and moaning.

"Yu have to hold his arm," I say, "or I can't get it into him."

Brady steadies his brother and I get the needle in without breaking it or the vein, even though the vampire howls, keens, and shakes his feet on the bed.

When I pull out the needle, the vampire quiets and breathes in gasps, staring at the ceiling. I wonder if he is having a bad reaction.

Arsen returns.

"We need to go. I just found out where Niko went. And you won't believe it."

CHAPTER 7

He's right. I don't believe it.

We are in the car driving back to the Draugur mansion, our mansion.

"Why the hell would he go to Boston?"

"It's one of the oldest cities in the United States and would be a place where Niko would have some holdings. It's relatively close to New York, so it would be easy for him to deploy the virus from there and spread it through the northeast. And he might think we wouldn't look for him in that town especially since it's not on the list where he has his holdings."

"And you got such a list where?"

"The Elders."

I shoot him a look.

"How do you think the Elders fund all their activities, Sasha? They tax us on what we own."

"What?"

"Don't be surprised. They call it tithing."

"And that's better?"

"It's the price of not having another faction go after you. Money paves the way for peace."

"Arsen, you blow my mind at least once every few hours."

He smiles slyly.

"I hope so."

"Everything is sex with you."

"Well, almost everything. And speaking of it, I have to arrange our ride."

I roll my eyes because it seems indeed every word that vaguely rings of sex seems to bring him around to that subject. Which isn't a bad thing, except we are in motion.

Arsen calls a private charter on his smartphone and arranges for a flight to Hartford. We wait a few minutes while the dispatcher checks on lift-off and landing windows, which is another thing I learn. You don't just pop into an airport, even a private one without having a certain time to leave and land.

"We can get you into New Haven tomorrow morning at five a.m. eastern time, which means you need to board by nine p.m. here. Should I book it?"

"Go ahead," says Arsen. They make a few arrangements, including a limo

"Nine? That's in a few hours."

"No time for courting. Sorry."

"But why so early?"

"With your big brain, I'd thought you'd know. Time zones, darling. There is a three-hour difference between here and the East Coast. So we do not have time to even take a bathroom break. We need to pack and get to the airport."

And everything is rush-rush. And when we get to the bedroom, I find a bunch of boxes with my name on it.

"What's this?"

"I had some of the boys pack up your things from your apartment. Sorry I didn't tell you, but you were complaining you didn't have clothes, and you would make the move anyway. I instructed them to label the boxes, but what you can't find, we'll buy when we get there."

The walls crash in around me and I sit on the bed. This is too much. My whole life has been dictated by someone else for the past month, and I have absolutely no say.

"I should stay here," I say.

Arsen stops packing a duffle and sits on the bed and puts his arm around me.

"I can't do this without you."

"Yes, you can. You've been doing it without me for centuries. I don't know what I'm doing, or why, or where I'm going, or what I will do when I get there."

"Hey," he says as he kisses my temple tenderly. "Where's that badass vampire who put Gheorghe in his place?"

"She's taken a hike and left me here."

"You're going to do fine. I'm sure Miss Badass will emerge when we need her. Is there anything I can get for you?"

"No. Wait. I should bring my notebook, just in case. I left it in the lab."

"I'll get it."

"No. You finish packing. I'm taking you up on a shopping trip because I don't have the heart to go through boxes now."

He smiles. "You got a deal."

So I run off to the lab to collect my notebook. I don't know if I need it or not, but it lends me a funky sense of security to know I do. And as I round the corner, I run into the one person I don't want to.

Claudette.

Surprised, she hisses at me—an honest-to-god, hiss.

"Watch it," she snarls.

"You're the one that needs to watch it. What the hell were you doing at Niko's compound?"

Her eyes narrow.

"What you are talking about?"

"You sure as hell do. I spotted you at the Baetal compound."

"You saw nothing."

"Sure I did. And Arsen did, too."

Her lips curl in eerie delight. "That is where you are wrong. If I was there, which I wasn't, Arsen would question me now. You overplayed your hand, just like you always do. One day, Arsen will see through you and discard you, just like every other woman."

Sometimes you want to smash someone in the face, and this was one of those times. But a fight would only get Arsen pissed at both of us.

"Suit yourself. I'll figure out what's going on. In my heart you are a traitor, Claudette. I can wait to get proof."

Claudette scoffs. "Go right ahead and collect your proof, fledgling. You see I'm quaking in my shoes."

She rolls her eyes and pushes past me, hurrying to get nowhere fast.

Fuck her. I've got other things to do. And once we leave this house, I won't have to deal with that vicious woman for a while, which makes going to Boston worthwhile.

When I return to the room, I find Jackson in deep discussion with Arsen, and for an irrational second, I feel left out."

"Hi," I say.

"Hey," says Jackson. "Okay, I'll meet you there."

"There?"

"Gotta go, Sasha. Arsen will fill you in."

Jackson rushes past me like he has something better to do than acknowledge me. Now I really feel left out or left behind.

"What was that about?"

"Jackson told me that he and some other vampire hunters got a tip that Niko was in Boston, like we thought. I feel better about going there now. They are taking a commercial flight and will be in Boston later tomorrow."

"Why don't they just come with us?"

Arsen gives me an indulgent glance. "Sasha, Jackson is fine hanging out with his sworn enemy but his compatriots are not."

"Oh, I guess." Still, it is weird to have Jackson ignore me and not even say a few words to me. It isn't like him at all.

More rushing, and Arsen shouts out orders to different people as we hurry to the car. Henri is driving us so we don't leave the car behind, and a rental is waiting for us in Boston. I settle back in the leather seat of the Lincoln Town Car, and Arsen takes my hand as Henri drives us to the airport.

Arsen reaches into the jacket he's wearing and hands me a black card.

"Here," he said. "For anything you want. No limit."

I turn it over.

"You're shitting me."

"No shit, Sasha."

"So, if I, like, want to buy a Porsche, this thing will go through?"

"It will, but why you would you need to? We have plenty of Porches."

"Not the point, Arsen. It's just I've had nothing like this before."

He draws me closer with his strong arms and kisses me.

"Stick with me, babe, and the sky's the limit."

"What? You haven't diversified to space travel yet? I hear all the cool billionaires do."

"Is that what it will take for you to consider me 'cool'? My vast diamond mines don't do it for you?"

"Diamond mines are passé."

"Well," he says, pursing his lips. "I'll consider it."

It isn't until we are on the plane, a light business-class Cessna, and in the air that we can relax.

"Do you want a drink? There is a fully stocked bar."

I yawn involuntarily. "It's been a busy day. I'd like to sleep."

"Go ahead. The seats tilt back, and I mean all the way."

I don't lay it flat but a comfortable sixty degrees, and it doesn't take long for me to go to sleep. But as I find out, sleeping in a moving plane, the little bumps and jolts that come from turbulence keeps me in a strange state.

I jolt awake seeing Arsen lying in his bed, and I'm confused. We are on a plane. But no. This is Arsen's room, and Arsen is so pale, his face is white and he shivers uncontrollably. He's dying and there is nothing I can do about it.

Niko swaggers into the room. "Well, I'm finished infecting all the vampires. All I have to do is wait." He glances casually at Arsen.

"Won't be long now. He'll die. Your bond will break and you'll be mine."

"No, you bastard. Where's the cure? You have one."

And he, incredibly sings an old Bee Gees song, "How Can You Mend a Broken Heart?"

"Stop it, stop it!" I scream. "You are no Barry Gibbs!"

I run to him and beat his chest.

"Stop it, stop it!"

"Sssh, sssh, sweetheart." It's Arsen's honey-gravel voice, but how can it be? Arsen's on the bed dying.

"Wake up, sweetheart, you are having a bad dream."

My eyes open and I find I'm on his lap and he's holding me, stroking my hair. And I breathe with relief that the awful thing I saw isn't happening.

"Some badass vampire, I am," I say. "Freaked out over a little dream."

"Dreams are important," says Arsen. "You can learn a lot from a dream. What did you see?"

"You, on the bed from a virus Niko made."

"Oh," he whispers.

"And Niko was singing a Bee Gees song."

He raises an eyebrow.

"He was? Which one was it?"

"'How Do You Mend A Broken Heart."

"I dimly remember it. But, how would you? You weren't born then."

"I had an aunt who was a big Bee Gees fan. Played their music all the time."

He pulls me closer to his chest.

"Well, I'd say this dream is very serious."

"You do?"

"Yes. It shows your abject fear of Bee Gees songs. Maybe there was some childhood trauma attached to one?"

I try to hit him, but he catches my hand with those super-fast reflexes of his and then nips my wrist, sending a shiver through me. Blood beads up and his tongue laps it up. "Mmmm, delicious."

"Are you hungry?" I ask. He fed yesterday and this morning, so he can't be hungry, not that fast.

"I'm always hungry for you, sweetheart."

His steely hard cock presses into my ass like a brand. He licks my wrist tenderly and I groan. He presses his lips to the mating mark on my neck, and I squirm on his lap.

"I want you," he whispers in my ear. It's a hot breeze that prickles and teases and just his words make me wet.

"Arsen," I breathe. He's too sexy and my brain has ceased thinking function and only the words "more" and "now" come to mind.

Vaguely I'm aware that there are two pilots in the forward cabin behind the shut hatch.

"I could have ordered a steward," he whispers. "But I wanted us to have the cabin to ourselves."

"Good planning," I say.

He unbuttons his shirt and pulls it aside.

"I want you to feed from me, here, close to my heart."

The idea shocks me. "Is that dangerous?"

"No. But I want to look down on your face and see your bliss as you suck."

I put my mouth to his pec above the nipple and let my fangs slice slowly into his flesh. He gasps. "Sasha, that is so delicious how you do that."

I drink, taking him in, his heart pulsing against my mouth, and his cock pressing into me and I moan.

"That's right, sweetheart." Arsen bends his head and kisses my neck, lapping it with his tongue. Sweet fire spreads through my neck as his fangs slice into my flesh. Our hearts beat in time as our blood flows from one to another. I wrap my arms around his neck, holding him closer, driving his fangs deeper. There is nothing that I do not want from this man. Time fades, and all that exists is the both of us locked in a deathly embrace, promising life.

Arsen moves under me and with his strong arms, pulls down my jeans and lifts me to pull his khakis down. His shaft rubs against my wet heat and I'm lost utterly. There isn't two people here, but two hearts joined as one.

He pushes up my hips and enters me by pulling them down on his cock. We cling to each other, rocking back and forth.

Fire builds in my core because his movements are so gently they just barely satisfied my need for friction. Slowly he bucks his hips and the rhythm of him moving within me is delightful torture. He keeps me hanging on the edge, every movement of his cock good and promising more.

My heart quickens, and I try to move my hips, but he holds them fast. My pleasure is his to command and he will give what I need at the appropriate time. I make a mental note to have a chat with him about this domineering streak of his, but right now I give into his demands. He pinches both ass cheeks sharply as he drives his cock in me, and with my mouth full of blood I can make no sound.

"Don't you dare spill a drop," he says roughly.

Holding my hips up he dives again and again into me roughly. His mouth is off my neck and he grunts each time he dives deeper inside as if he's trying to find a long-buried treasure. Arsen is splitting me apart, and I can no longer keep my mouth on him. I pull away, licking me lips, careful not to waste any of his blood. I jam my hips down on his steel-within-velvet cock, until I'm past pain, past pleasure and climbing in a space that is only heat and need.

"Come for me, baby," he says. "Come, Sasha!"

All that I am bursts apart in little pieces, and I'm flying through the universe, no longer separate from anything.

With one final spearing thrust, Arsen groans and lets loose within me. His heat fills me and consumes me until we both finally still, holding each other with his cock still inside me.

I don't know how long we sit like this. I may have dozed off and he might have as well. The next thing I know, a voice crackles over the plane's intercom.

"We're about to land. Please strap into your seats."

"Well, we better get ourselves together, or," he smiles at me, "we'll never get off this plane."

My mouth opens. "Do you think he heard?"

Arsen gives me a wicked smile as if he just talked with the devil and got an answer he liked.

"Sweetheart, there is only one reason a client declines a steward."

"Now you tell me."

CHAPTER 8

The beauty about Boston is that Logan International Airport is close to the city proper, and it is very easy to get into the city from it. The hell about Boston is that once you get inside, it is nearly impossible to move around it.

"I should have hired a car and driver," says Arsen, frustrated with the constant log jams and detours because of the continuous roadwork of this major city.

"We'll keep that in mind the next time we come here."

"There won't be a next time. There is a reason I don't come to Boston often."

"Traffic?"

"No. Bad luck. It follows me everywhere here."

"Arsen, the scientist in me says there is no such thing as bad luck."

"And me the man who has had to flee for my life more than once from Boston says otherwise."

"You should have told me. We could have sent someone else."

"No," he says, stubbornly. "I mean to put an end to this nonsense with Niko. He's gone off the deep end. Rivalry is one thing. Slaughtering whole covens is another. I'm going to end him one way or the other, regardless of the consequences."

"Wait, there will be consequences?"

"He's the Baetal prince. Of course there will be consequences. Hopefully we've documented his crimes enough that should I have to kill him, it will stand up in a tribunal."

Now I'm getting frightened.

"Arsen, what would happen to you if a tribunal decides his killing wasn't justified?"

"Then they'll kill me."

"No!"

He pats my hand while we sit at a stoplight. "But that won't happen. Why do you think you are with me?"

"Because I'm irresistible?"

He smiles. "Well, that too. It's because Niko is your maker and you should have a natural allegiance to him."

"Well, I don't."

"That's because I made you feed from me right away."

"Wait? Are you admitting you manipulated the situation?"

"Sasha, understand I did it with the best of intentions. If I got you into my coven, then Niko didn't have sole control of the only cure we knew."

"Arsen!"

"What did you expect me to do? My people were sick and the only one who got well was Niko after drinking your blood. Ah, here it is, the entrance to the highway."

Arsen casually swings onto the highway, making some progress while we drive deeper into the city. I see signs for places I've only heard about. Harvard. Fenway Park. But I'm not in the mood for sightseeing. I'm pissed, and he knows it. And I shouldn't be, and he knows that, too. I had told him I wanted him to tell me everything, and now that he does, I'm ticked to find out all his ulterior motives. And it's not like I didn't suspect he kept his true machination to himself, but I really hate this manipulative part of Arsen.

We pull into an area that is less commercial with older and graceful buildings. Mansions of another era sit in neat-like street blocks. We pull into the driveway of an especially large house. The air about it is dark and forbidding and I notice humans walking past giving us furtive glances and hurry by.

"What is this place?"

"It's a chapter house."

"Say what?"

"Different factions keep houses in the larger cities for their visiting members. We find that it is a convenient way to keep problems at bay. Each house keeps a certain number of thralls for feeding. It keeps the police out of our business. This is the Boston Draugur Chapter House."

I shove my hands in my pocket, not liking this idea at all.

"What do these thralls get out of this?"

"We treat them very well. They get free food, housing, and the education of their choice. If you notice, we are in the middle of Harvard country. Most of our thralls go to Harvard."

"So," I say, sourly, "it's no worse than selling your blood for cash."

"Come inside, Sasha. I think you need some rest."

The inside is gorgeous, all gilt painted in the cornices and expensive Oriental rugs throughout. Dark wainscoting panel goes halfway up the walls and the ornate molding frames the doorways. Burgundy velvet wallpaper shot with gold graces the walls.

"Well back, Lord Eskandar," says a butler at the door.

"Jameson, this is Sasha Keleterina, my mate."

If Jameson is surprised, he doesn't show it.

"It is an honor to meet you, Lady Eskandar."

If there is anything I learned, it is to keep my mouth shut when someone makes a mistake like this.

"Thank you, Jameson."

"Is there," says Arsen, "a thrall in service tonight?"

"Yes, sir. Both fresh."

"One of them a male?"

"Yes, my lord."

"Send them both to my rooms."

"Very good, sir."

"And see what clothes we have for Ms. Keleterina, will you? Size two?" he asks me and I nod my head sullenly.

"I can send out to a personal shopper, my lord. It is a new service we have."

"Fine. Fetch whatever the shopper suggests, for casual wear, sleeping, and underwear. We do not expect to be staying long."

I am not happy. I cannot believe Arsen will drink from a thrall in front of me. I'm sullen as we climb the wide staircase to a suite of rooms on the second floor. I know we can't drink from each other solely all the time, but it's still hard to think of it. It is an intimate act, and I can't imagine sharing blood from someone just for food.

It is bigger than my apartment at school and much more luxurious. The sitting room alone is as large as a small house, and two bedrooms, one on each side of the sitting room, is almost as large. Each bedroom has an en suite bath.

"Nice," I concede.

Arsen answers the knock on the door and one man and one woman, both about my age stand in the doorway.

"Come in," says Arsen.

"Lord Eskandar, I'm William," says the man.

"And I'm Susan," says the female. "We are pleased to be of service."

"Susan, do me a favor and go to the bedroom there. I'll be in shortly."

"Thank you, Lord Eskandar."

"William, my mate, Sasha, is a new vampire. So far, she's

resisted taking a meal from a living body. Give her plenty of time to do so."

William nods solemnly.

"Of course, my lord."

"If she is stubborn, then call me."

"As you wish."

Arsen starts for the bedroom and I grab his arm.

"You can't be serious."

"But I am. It will not always be convenient to get you a bag of blood from a donation center, and this is how we feed."

"But you want me to pop my vampire cherry on someone I don't know?"

"Would you rather it was Jackson?"

"God, no." The idea horrifies me.

"Well then, be grateful it is with someone who knows what he is doing and why."

"But, but . . ."

Arsen sighs. "I'm going to eat and you will, too. We need our strength for what we will do tomorrow."

"But you are going in there with a woman."

"Your point being? Do you think I want anyone by you?"

"Well, no."

"We can switch up and you take the woman if you like. But it usually easier for fledglings to take from the opposite sex at first until you get used to it." He gives me a quick kiss. "Now, have your supper, and then we can go to bed."

Supper. He calls a man supper. How I can ever get used to this?

William watches me with placid eyes. "You must be hungry, mistress. You are looking pale. Come sit next to me."

He pats his hand on the sofa on which he sits and I move reluctantly to that spot.

"Arsen tells me that you go to Harvard?"

"Yes, ma'am. Harvard Law."

"And this is a great opportunity?"

"The work is easy and gives me plenty of time to concentrate on my studies. This chapter house is not used much, and if I donate a couple times a month, that's rare."

"You have to be careful on how much you give."

"That's why there are four of us here on a rotating basis."

"I see." Arsen and crew seems to have this system worked out perfectly. Everyone is on board. No one is coerced or assaulted. The well-compensated thralls seem in perfect command of their free will. Why then, does this seem so awful?

"You will not hurt me, not appreciably," says William, raising his arm. "Can I tell you a secret?"

I nod my head.

"I like it. You all are so powerful. I hope one day that a Draugur will take me into the clan."

I move to pull away because I thoroughly dislike his words. Someone aspires to be a vampire? That is a horrible thought. But William will not let go of my hand. He moves his wrist to press it against my mouth and the vein on his wrist pulses. The scent of his blood seeps through his skin.

"Good ahead," he says. "I want you to."

Instinct overcomes common sense, and my fangs descend and slice into his flesh. Blood flows and I suck it in, deep and rich and satisfying, and William moans at the ferocity of my taking.

"Take it. Take it all," murmurs William.

"Sasha!" Arsen's voice cuts through my bloodlust. He pulls William's wrist down and off my fangs, and he pushes me back from sucking on the wrist once more.

"Okay," he said. "Cherry popped. I guess that won't be a problem anymore." He lifts the handset of the phone. "Jameson, William needs help to get to his room. Also, he needs liquids and iron supplements."

"I'm fine," slurs William.

"You will not argue with me. And if you wish to continue with this arrangement, you will do what you are told. No activity today and tomorrow. Rest, and food and liquids only."

Jameson knocks and enters, and between him and Susan they walk a weakened William out of the room.

Once the door is closed, I turn my primitive ire on Arsen.

"Why did you do that? He didn't have a problem with what I was doing!"

"Look at you. One minute you can't consider it, the next you can't wait to kill a thrall."

"Kill?" I say. I sit heavily on the sofa and cover my hands. "Oh my god. I almost killed a man."

Arsen puts his arm around me. "Sssh, sssh. This moment happens to everyone. With practice, you'll learn when to stop. I should have been with you, but I was afraid you'd be self-conscious if I stayed."

"I would," I admit. "Oh god, that was a close call, wasn't it?"

"No. I caught you in time. For extreme cases, we have procedures to help a thrall recover. He wasn't even near that point."

"Arsen, he wants to become a vampire. He kept saying, take it, take it all."

"And you mustn't, ever. Only Masters and Princes can make new vampires. It's our law. If you were to drain a human, you must let him die. Otherwise you would be subject to a death sentence, and," he says with a smile, "I'd hate that."

"Oh, god, Arsen. What would I do without you?"

"Exactly my point, sweetheart."

CHAPTER 9

I am a shameless hussy vampire because the next morning I'm doing my best to seduce Arsen. A satisfied hunger and a good night's sleep changes my perspective. William might be wonky in his desire to become a vampire, but he is getting a first-class law education. But I don't want to dwell on William now. My attention is laser-focused on one super sexy vampire who for once is not cooperating.

"Come on, baby," I urge as I put my hand on his thick shaft through the maddening pants he wears. "Need you."

Part of the problem is that Arsen is taking one long drink from me, which makes me squirm against him, panting with need, needing him inside me. I jut my hips against his and pull on his delicious ass, and I'm insane from needing him and not getting what I want.

I unbutton his pants and slide my hand inside. The feel of his cock is delightful, especially when it is hard. It is a kind of magic how this part of the male anatomy springs to life, pulsing, the skin as soft as silk but rigid and demanding. Why doesn't the bastard just give it up?

I am totally wet now, ready and waiting for him, and the heat between my legs is nearly unbearable. I growl in my frustration. "Give it up, already."

Arsen pulls away and kisses me, deep and long, perhaps to reassure me of his feelings in the matter. "And I need you, too. We'll have plenty of time to celebrate after we capture Niko."

My face burns and my breathing is shallow and all Arsen can think about is asshole Niko who has signed his own death warrant. Now I'm getting angry, partly from frustration and partly because in my mind I'm done with Niko. Let the other vampires take care of him. I don't understand why Arsen makes Niko's capture his personal mission.

"And that's our plan? You said you want to kill him."

"In the best of all worlds, I do. But I have to make a good try at capturing him. If he comes along willingly, then I'll bring him to the Elder Council and they can decide what to do with him."

"You will get Niko on a plane and across the country?"

"I've already planned for his transportation this morning while you were soaking in the tub."

"There are no flies on you? Is there?"

"I hope not," he says, with mock horror.

I'm still not copacetic with leaving this room and pursuing Niko instead of carnal pleasures. However, if doing so will get Arsen's attention back where it needs to be, ergo fucking me silly, then I'm for it.

"Well, then lead the way, my lord. Let's capture us a vampire and get on with the celebrating."

"Sounds like a plan."

"Where do we look?"

"The Baetal Chapter House. It's close to here. We can walk."

I'm shocked. Niko can be that close and Arsen is acting cool about it?

"And you think he's there, why?"

"Simple. He's always been a cheap bastard. He won't spend

money he doesn't have to. If he's not there, I have more places to look."

We walk through Cambridge and both sides of the street have sidewalks as if it is expected that everyone will walk. Cars park on a single side of the road attest to the lack of parking here. Some houses have old-fashioned hitching posts for horses at the gates or at the curb. All the Victorian buildings are similar in age and style. Some are grander than others, but I have the sense of a place stuck in time, uncaring whether the world marches past it or not.

Arsen slows before we reach a large white mansion with Grecian columns holding up the front porch.

"Is that it?"

He nods.

"Not ostentatious at all, is it?" I say, sarcastically.

"The Baetal have always had an overboard sense of style."

"So what do we do?"

"You walk in and ask to speak to Niko."

"Me?"

"You're Baetal, right? They'll scent you belong."

"Like each clan has its own scent?"

"Haven't you noticed?"

"Well, no. Arsen, I swear each day I'm with you I feel like there is a bunch of stuff I should have a clue about that I don't."

"You'll learn."

"And what about you?"

"I'll hang out by the door. I've drunk enough of your blood that they should not recognize me as Draugur at first."

"That is why you were driving me crazy?"

"Yes," he says, simply, and I want to smash him.

"I'm going to forget that you fed off me this morning for camouflage."

"It's not the only reason. You are delicious."

I roll my eyes. "Just walk in there?"

"It's our best shot."

I move forward, regretting each step, and hesitate at the door. I look over my shoulder and Arsen nods, egging me on. I raise the doorknocker, and with my first strike the door creaks open.

"Hello?" I say.

No answer. It is eerie quiet. Plus, I smell a horrible scent.

"Arsen," I say, waving him forward. "Come here."

"What's up?"

"That smell. O' de Baetal?"

"The scent of dead vampire."

"You sure?"

He nodded with his jaw set. "Positive."

"Niko? Someone got to him?"

Arsen shrugs. "Let's find out."

He walks ahead of me and moves quickly through the room on the first floor while I stand as a lookout.

Arsen returns and shakes his head.

"No one here. I don't scent a single live Baetal."

"Well, hell of a homecoming," I say. "What happened?"

"No clue. But the dead vampire would be one."

Slowly we climb the wide-centered stairs to the second floor, scanning for sudden movements, and letting our noses lead us to the dead vamp. Arsen opens the door and his body stiffens.

"Holy hell," he says. "I will fucking kill him."

"What?" I say as I push forward. I can't imagine what would get Arsen this upset until I see the vampire sprawled lifeless on the bed.

Red blood spills from where a stake stabbed her heart. Surprise and horror fix her face in a terrible rictus, wide eyes glassy without sight, and her mouth opened in a scream. This is a horrible enough sight but who lies there is worse.

Claudette.

Arsen's face turns beet red as he rushes forward. That's when I see it, visible only from a glint of sunlight racing from the window along a silver wire—a tripwire stretches across the floor.

"No!" I cry as I rush forward. Then I hear a click and Arsen does, too. He stops and freezes his movements.

"Get out of here, Sasha."

"No. I'm not leaving you here alone."

"You have to go. This will blow."

"No," I say, stubbornly. "Do you not understand? We are together, always. In life. In death. So you damn well better figure a way out of this mess because I cannot live an immortal life without you. I'd rather die."

He looks at me and the wire just under his foot and I know he can't extract it without setting off the bomb.

"You would?"

I nod my head.

"Then come here, babe. Slowly."

I do it because I understand. We'll go out together. It has to be this way. He grabs me with a grip as tight as a vise.

"Hang on," he says.

I should know that Arsen is this strong, but it always amazes me the things that he does. He springs up, dragging me along and then twists to slam through the glass window at the side of the room.

Heat, smoke, and glass chase us as a large boom shatters the peace of the neighborhood. We tumble and twist in the air debris following our trajectory out and down to the lawn the below. Arsen lands first, holding me tightly, taking the brunt of the fall.

The building explodes once again, this time into flames. Arsen sits up, clutching me tightly.

"Are you okay?" he asks, urgently.

"I'm fine. You are a soft place to land."

Arsen looks around furtively, and I spot the curious stepping from their homes at the same time he does.

"We've got to go."

"No argument here," I say.

I clutch Arsen's arm as we run through Cambridge, even as the blaring of fire engine horns and squeal of police cars surround us. But I don't hold on to him for me but for him. Arsen's face is white, and he keeps mumbling, "Murderer, murderer," and I am anxious for him. I don't think it is a good idea for Arsen to show up at the Draugur house in this state. He already has enough problems with vampires in our neck of the woods who think he is weak. We don't need that on this side of the country, too. I look around for a place to stop as we stumble onto a main drag lined with a bunch of storefronts. I spot a coffee shop.

"Let's stop there," I say. "I need a drink."

Arsen is in no condition to argue. Seeing Claudette like that, with a wooden stake in her heart, rattles him thoroughly. When we walk in, I dash us to the bathrooms.

"Get cleaned up. I'll get us some coffee."

After ducking in the ladies' room and doing a quick washup, I walk to the counter and order up some venti lattes. This is the first time I use the magic credit card Arsen gave me. I spent a few anxious moments waiting for Arsen to come out of the restroom and briefly wondered if I should extract him. But finally the door cracks open, and Arsen, looking a small measure better, joins me at the table.

He picks at the paper holder on the cup and says nothing for a long time.

I touch his arm, looking for a reaction or reassurance.

"Arsen?"

Arsen huffs. "She was mine," he says in the darkest tone I ever heard from his mouth.

I dislike that he says this, but for his sake, I keep my mouth shut. He doesn't need my jealousy right now. He is not taking this well, and I can't help but think how much worse it will be if he lost his sister.

"I was her master," Arsen says hoarsely, "Niko had no business murdering her like that."

He holds his head down, his eyelids lowered and I cannot see his eyes.

"She betrayed you. She was the one feeding Niko all that information about us."

"You can't know that," he says with venom in his words.

"Why was she here? In Boston? I told you I saw her walk out of Niko's compound. You dismissed me."

Arsen reaches out his hand and takes mine.

"If I dismissed you, I am sorry. Claudette, for all her faults, devoted her life to the clan."

"No. She loved you. And you turned her away. What's worse is that you mated me. You left her no options. She turned to the one vampire she thought could help her in her quest to win you back. Your enemy."

Arsen looks away and sighs. "I suppose."

"The problem is Niko is still twisting in the wind, and he knows we tracked him down. He'll be twice as hard to catch."

He nods, staring into his coffee.

"A stake," he mutters. "A fucking stake. He knew we were coming, and he did that."

"Arsen," I say, gently, "he did it because Claudette told him we were coming."

"Don't tell me," he says, as his eyes flash with anger, "that it was her own fault she died."

This is not doing any good, and I have to get Arsen to focus on something else.

"Arsen? Who is taking care of your sister now if Claudette isn't with her?"

"Well, any number of people."

"Don't you think you should check on that? Because if Claudette slipped away to make a clandestine trip to Boston, maybe she wouldn't raise red flags by arranging your sister's care with someone else."

Arsen's expression turns from remorse to concern, from zero to sixty flat, and he whips out his phone.

"Henri, Arsen. Who is with my sister now?"

His mouth forms a tight line.

"No. It is not Claudette. Ask around. When was the last anyone saw Claudette? No. I'll wait."

Arsen sips his coffee grimly while he waits for Henri to answer. I watch him carefully. I have never seen him like this, so on edge and close to losing control. What would I do if Arsen goes into a rage as vampires can do? Well, humans can, too, but they don't have a vampire's supernormal strength, and a deadly capacity to deal death when it suits them.

I am no match for Arsen, and in this moment, my inadequacies tear at me like a scavenger at a piece of carrion. Much of this is my fault, and I am at a loss as to how to make any of this right. I do not regret Claudette's death. She was an annoyance, and a troublemaker, and she cared more about her own agenda than for her people. Her only saving grace and her downfall was she loved Arsen. But her passion twisted into ugly circumstances driving her to desperate acts.

I pull out my phone and check the commercial flights to Boston.

Arsen lifts his head.

"Okay. Thank you. Tell the rest that Claudette is dead. We found her in the Baetal Chapter House. Yes. Baetal. And arrange for some people to care for my sister. Thank you, Henri."

Arsen puts his phone down slowly on the table.

"No one saw her after we left."

"There is a commercial flight to Boston in the evening. She would have gotten here ahead of us. But Arsen, that means she'd have been planning this before we decided to leave."

Arsen's expression grows grimmer. "She used the commotion

of us leaving to hide her departure." He raises his hand and smashes it on the table. The other patrons of the coffee shop turn their heads toward us.

"Bitch!" he says.

The alarm siren in my head rings double time now. I never heard Arsen refer to a woman with any pejorative. I lay my hand on top of his.

"Arsen, I won't tell you to calm down."

"Good," he says, curtly. His eyes glow now, not a good thing in the middle of a crowded coffeehouse, and I'm desperate to cool him down. Arsen is a countdown away from a major firework display. It cannot happen here where humans would see a preternatural creature spilling his ire on the world at large.

"We should go," I say. Maybe I can get him to walk this off.

But his phone rings, and he picks it up. Hs expression turns even darker.

"Good," he says. "We'll meet you there."

He looks at me with a gaze so cutting, I shiver.

"That was Jackson. He's in town. One of his sources said Niko will be at an event in town. It's probably why he came here."

Here we go with the "shit Sasha doesn't know" again. This is probably some super-secret vampire convention that every vamp knows about but me. This is getting old.

"What event?"

"You'll see," Arsen says. He grabs my hand.

"Let's go. I want to scout out the best position to observe Niko."

CHAPTER 10

The street is packed with people, tight as a Manhattan train at rush hour. The party where Niko was sighted has spilled out into the city at large and taken over. The atmosphere fairly vibrates with excitement. The air is full of the scent of sweat and sex and alcohol and the deep, bone-shaking rattle of bass so intense, you can't hear the rest of the music. Not that anyone here seems to care.

The buildings of this old, neglected district crowd close to the road, but the spaces between them have been strung with lights and flags by the enthusiastic partygoers, for whom this fun night out seems to have evolved into a Dionysian revel. The lights cast a Sulphur-yellow glow on the world like an old photograph. There is alcohol in everyone's hands and on the pavement and sticky hoods of cars and splashed on every wall. Weed and ecstasy are shared as freely as the booze, and it isn't hard to find the acid and cocaine once I look for it. It's a legendary party, and one I'd love to be part of, if I didn't have more violent delights on my mind.

"I thought this was supposed to be a rave?" Arsen says, moving through the crowd with surprising grace for a man of his size. "Feels more like Mardi Gras."

"I'm surprised Jackson's contacts spotted anyone in this mob," I say, following him with slightly less success. Someone drops his beer and I barely dodge getting soaked. "You seeing anything?"

He shakes his head.

"Crowd's too thick!" He shouts to be heard over the music. "He could be standing right next to us, and I wouldn't know."

He's right. Even my vampire senses are useless in all this. All I can hear is the bass and the joyful shrieking, and my nose is full of the scent of piss and beer.

"Maybe if we get a little higher," Arsen suggests. "We could climb on that car?"

"And make ourselves targets?" I point out. "No. We're not going to get anywhere searching like this. Let's split up. I'll take the north side of the street, you take the south. We'll regroup when Jackson and his hunters show up."

"We should stay together," Arsen says, frowning hard. He stops walking, interrupting the flow of the crowd. A couple of people throw him dirty looks, but he's big and intimidating enough that most people just slide around him like a boulder in a stream. He crosses his arms over his broad chest.

"Arsen, don't be ridiculous," I say, not backing down. I mimic his posture, arms crossed. "We won't cover enough ground together, and you know it. I'm not planning to tackle the asshole on my own the minute I see him. But if we're going to get the weasely little son of a bitch, we need to be smart."

He tries to stare me down for a minute, but I know I'm right. He breaks first, looking away.

"I just don't want you getting hurt," he admits, barely audible over the thunderous music. "After almost losing you, can you blame me for not wanting to let you out of my sight?"

I smile, stepping a little closer to touch his cheek.

"I'm a big girl, Arsen," I tell him softly. "I can tie my own shoes and everything. I'll be all right."

He smiles back at me, covering my hand with his own.

"I know you will," he says. "I underestimated you once and it nearly cost me everything. I won't make that mistake again. I know you can handle yourself. I just don't want you to need to."

He laces our fingers and pulls my hand to his mouth to press a soft kiss in my palm.

"I'm not going to hold you back," he promises. "I don't think I could if I tried, honestly. You're a goddamn force of nature."

"Damn right I am," I reply, proudly.

"Just don't ask me to stop trying to look out for you," he pleads. "I've got your back, always."

"I know you do," I say, and I pull him closer into a brief, warm kiss. My heart flutters with giddy happiness at the change in his attitude. I don't mind him wanting to protect me. But that he's willing to respect my strength is so much more important.

We split up and I move to the edges of the crowd, staying near the buildings and keeping an eye out not just for Niko but for Jackson as well. I scan the buildings for a convenient fire escape or balcony to climb and get an overhead view. I spot a likely one, but there's a couple not-so-discreetly fucking right next to it and I can't bring myself to interrupt them.

"Hey. Hey bitch!" Someone in the crowd yells. "You in the tight-ass leather pants!"

I spare a glance in the stranger's direction, just to make sure it isn't someone I know. It isn't. It's some random partygoer of the white-guy-with-dreads variety. I quickly look away, but he seems to have taken the millisecond of my attention as encouragement to continue.

"You alone?" he demands with a brainless grin. "Babe, your ass looks amazing in those pants. Let me get my face up in those cheeks. I won't come out for days."

I stare at a brick wall in the opposite direction from the asshole and keep walking.

"Hey, hey bitch! Come back!" the guy begs. "I got a tab of Molly with your name on it! You don't even gotta let me touch the ass, just let a guy look, man!"

I contemplate interrupting the couple fucking in front of the fire escape ladder just for the sake of getting away from this noisy asshole. He isn't the first guy to holler at me tonight, but he's probably the most annoying. I ignore him, which is generally the best course of action with this kind of dickbag, and focus on my mission, searching the crowd for familiar faces and the buildings for decent vantage points.

A hand grabs my hip and for a moment I think the catcalling asshole has progressed to actual assault, in which case I fully intend to feed him his own teeth. I realize I've guessed incorrectly when the hand spins me around with shocking strength. Niko smiles at me with sharp teeth and undisguised malice.

"Hello, beautiful."

"Just the man I was looking for," I snarl, reaching for a weapon.

"Careful," Niko says, and I feel the sharp point of a stake against my back. "We wouldn't want anyone's hand to slip."

I slowly let my hand fall away from the hilt of my knife, my mouth twisted with sour regret. I don't know what pisses me off more. That he snuck up on me or that I haven't stabbed him for it yet.

"Good girl," Niko says, which instantly takes the cake for things pissing me off the most right now. "Let's enjoy the party, shall we?"

He takes my right hand in his right, his left still at my lower back with the stake, like he's about to escort me onto a dance floor. Instead he leads me into the crush of the crowd. I scan quickly for Arsen, hoping I can signal him discreetly. I glimpse him, or someone who looks like him, for just a second through the crowd but he doesn't see me.

"I don't know what you're planning," I tell Niko. "But I'm not leaving this party with you."

"Well that would be a shame," Niko says lightly, digging the stake a little harder into my back. "It would be a shame for all these nice people around, us too. Collateral damage is such a sad inevitability, isn't it?"

That's it. I won't put up with him threatening a bunch of innocent strangers.

I dig my heels in, forcing him to come to a stop. The stake stabs into my back almost hard enough to draw blood, but I ignore it. He frowns at me and I meet his eyes. I want him to know how deadly serious I am.

"Do it," I tell him. "Or let me go. You can end all of this now, one way or another."

There's a strange look in his eyes at my brazen demand. He almost, for a moment, seems sorry for the path we've taken.

"This will only end one of two ways," he tells me, and his playful malice has been replaced by a dreadful certainty. "I will succeed, or I will die."

"It doesn't have to be that way," I insist, a strange pity squeezing my heart. He is my maker, after all. And I don't like the thought of anyone marching needlessly to his death. "There's still time to change things."

Niko laughs, and the moment of severity is gone, his devil-may-care smile returning.

"Darling," he says with faux affection. "I would never have begun this endeavor if I was not fully willing to gamble my life on it. I'm prepared to die. Are you?"

A burst of light and noise interrupts our conversation. There are cheers from the crowd. Someone's setting off fireworks. They explode above us, casting everything below in shades of red, green, and silver. Niko stares up at them, and the surprised wonder on his face is almost enough to make me forget that he's a murderous monster. Almost.

I grab the wrist holding the stake with one hand and with the other drive my elbow into his solar plexus hard enough that I hear the wind rush out of his lungs. He wheezes, bending over me, but keeps a solid grip on my arm. Solid enough that I can't pull away. So I stay in close, twisting and digging my sharp nails into the tender point of his wrist until he drops the stake into my waiting free hand. I jerk it toward his chest, but not fast enough. He catches my arm, twists it behind my back, and takes the stake. As he swings it toward my ribs, still gripping my wrist, I slam my heel into his knee and hear him gasp in pain. That would have inverted the joint of a human, but it hurts almost as much for a vampire. I kick it again for good measure, wrench my arm out of his grip and go for one of my knives. But I've barely got my fingers around the handle before he wraps both arms around me, pinning my arms to my sides and dragging me back against him. His hips grind against my ass hard enough to make my breath catch. He laughs, soft and breathy against my ear.

"Why Sasha, if you missed me that much you only had to say so."

Rage boils in my veins, evaporating any brief pity I might have felt for this fucking ambulatory skid mark in the jock strap of the world's most hygiene-averse high school football player. I'm contemplating the most efficient way to rip his dick off and beat him with it when I hear a telltale whistle in the air, easily lost among the scream of the fireworks and the roar of the crowd. I duck, slipping down out of Niko's grip, a second before a silver knife slams into his shoulder, sending him reeling backward. I straighten up, grinning as I see who threw it. Jackson readies a second knife, Arsen beside him, looking pissed enough to tear Niko apart with his bare hands.

"I had that handled," I tell them. "But thank you."

"Any time," Jackson says, graciously. "But the night ain't over yet."

He gestures behind me, where Niko is making a tactical retreat, dropping the silver knife he just ripped out of his shoulder behind him as he barrels through the crowd, knocking people aside in his pain and haste.

I pick up the silver knife with a grin and gesture to Jackson and Arsen.

"Come on boys. Let's go kill this son of a bitch."

CHAPTER 11

I sprint after Niko, shoving people out of the way as I struggle to close the distance between us. He's moving fast. Much faster than I expect. Was he holding back when we raced during the tournament? Or maybe it's just desperation. Even when he's out of my sight, I can smell the tang of his blood on the air, cutting through the stink of booze and human bodies. A cut from a silver knife won't heal quickly. He knows it, and he knows he won't be getting away from me. Which means he is definitely going to try some stupid bullshit. I need to get out of this crowd, both for the sake of speed and in hopes of avoiding collateral damage.

I shove my way to the side of the crowd and vault up onto a fire escape, flying up the metal toward the roof, barely touching the steps. Big upside to vampirism—instant parkour master. The senses heightened by the transformation aren't just sight and smell, after all. My sense of balance is better, my depth perception more accurate. Unfortunately, even the vampire virus can't give you the benefits of experience. Niko has the same heightened senses as I do, and he's been using them a lot longer. Still, there's nothing quite like the sensation of flying over the rooftops, leaping from building to building, dragging yourself up by your fingertips or your core muscles alone, with absolute unshakable faith in the power of your own body. It almost makes all the other bullshit worth it, honestly.

I spot Niko, still down on the street but moving fast, employing the same skills I am as he vaults from cement barrier to car roof to parking meter to bike railing like an acrobat on speed. My fingers itch for my knives or better yet a gun, but I can't risk it while he's surrounded by innocent people. Which is exactly why he's still down there. Asshole.

I see something in my peripheral and risk a glance to the side. On the other side of the street, Arsen is vaulting across the roof tops as well, keeping pace with me. When all this is over, I want to race him again. Or better yet, just let him chase me and see how long it takes him to catch me, and how worked up I can get him before he does.

But for the moment I'm just glad he's beside me, going after the same goal, the asshole currently crashing through an unfortunate hot dog cart. *Hope you got covered in hot dog water, douchebag. Hope you never get the smell out.*

Glancing back, I can see Jackson in the distance, followed by several rough-looking strangers, presumably his other hunters. But he won't be catching up in time. I've learned firsthand that Jackson is nothing to fuck with, but a human can never hope to match a vampire in pure speed.

Up ahead, the party thins out as the street turns into an old jumper's bridge crossing a deep waterway. There's still a few handful of people hanging out across its length, but it's just the opening we need to grab Niko while he's clear of bystanders. I trade a glance with Arsen, who I know has come to the same conclusion. We drop down from the rooftops just before we run out of building and run on foot toward the bridge. We're already closing the distance. Niko's time is running out.

He glances back, and I expect to see fear in his eyes, the knowledge that he's about to be pile-drived into the asphalt by two hundred pounds of angry Draugur muscle. Instead, I see a cruel grin that makes my heart drop.

There are two teenagers, kids, leaning on the railing of the bridge, sipping beers they aren't old enough to have, laughing about some dumb joke. One freckled and redheaded and gangly, the other heavy set with thin blond hair. Just kids having a great evening. Until Niko grabs them both by the backs of their shirts, lifts them as easily as kittens, and chucks them both over the side of the bridge.

I hesitate for only a fraction of a second, but it would have been a fraction too long if it weren't for vampire speed. The bridge is too high. Those kids won't survive hitting the water. I have a choice, but it's no choice at all.

I don't even realize Arsen has made the same decision I have until I'm leaping over the side and I see him jumping after me. The dark water rushes up toward us like a freight train. The kids have barely processed what is happening, their eyes wide and limbs flailing. I'm just praying the fall is long enough for me to catch up as I narrow myself into diving posture, like a thrown dart, decreasing air resistance.

I catch the blond kid maybe a half second before we hit the water, but it's just long enough to pull him to my chest and turn, hitting the water with the flat of my back. It hurts like a motherfucker. At that distance, at that speed, water feels just as solid as concrete. It knocks the wind out of me, dazes me for a minute. I almost lose my grip on the kid. I struggle to get my senses back as we sink into the deep-green black of the water. The kid is out. I don't know if it is the stress or if I don't absorb enough of the shock from impact to protect him. My chest tightens into a vice of fear at the possibility of the latter, and the adrenaline is enough to help me shake off the daze. I grab the kid by the arms and kick for the surface. If you've ever swam too far out, or been grabbed by a riptide, and had to fight your way back to shore against the current, you know how exhausting it can be, even for a vampire. Especially if you're dragging an unconscious person. Lifeguards aren't ripped for nothing.

I drag myself and the kid up onto the gravelly bank and collapse, catching my breath. My whole back is one big throbbing bruise. If it weren't for vampire healing I would be feeling this for days. It's still going to suck for a few hours, at least.

Arsen beaches himself beside me, towing the redheaded kid. Thank God. I could never have caught them both on my own. I take a deep breath to still my shaking and sit up. We can't afford to lie here, as much as I'd like to. I check the blond kid's pulse, then roll him onto his side and give him a good few thumps on the back. He coughs up some green river water, sucks in a great deep breath, then curls up, moaning.

"How's that one?" I ask Arsen, pointing to his redhead.

"Breathing," Arsen replies, lifting his head from the kid's chest. "I think they're all right."

"Great," I say, heart still racing, and lean back on my hands, the gravel stabbing my palms. "Any chance Niko's still on that bridge, gloating?"

"Unless he's monologuing to the air like a comic book supervillain," Arsen flops onto his back, exhausted. "Probably not."

"Soliloquy."

An unfamiliar voice makes us both turn to look at the steep embankment behind us, where Jackson and his hunters are picking their way down. The comment came from a tall, rail-thin hunter I don't recognize, whose general aura is of a man who spends his weekends catfish noodling.

"Ain't a monologue if there's no one to listen," the man says with a Louisiana drawl that's too strong to possibly be genuine. "Monologue is delivered to other characters in the scene. He's just yackin' for no one but the audience, it's a soliloquy."

"Don't mind Rhett," Jackson says, patting the hunter on the shoulder and moving closer. "He's a fount of useless information."

"Got a bunch a those fact-a-day calendars," Rhett says, as though this explains anything.

"Nice catch, by the way," Jackson says, kneeling to check on the blond kid, who's still pretty out of it.

"Thanks," I say with a sigh. "But I'm pretty sure we've lost Niko."

"We'll get him," Jackson says, reassuringly. "He's still bleeding. We can pick up the trail, get an idea of what direction he went, at least."

"Ain't never seen a vampire do that," Rhett adds, and I blink at him in mild confusion. "Risk anything for a human like that. I mean, I'm guessing you knew you wouldn't die or nothing. But you must have known you'd lose that Niko fucker. Self-sacrifice ain't behavior I'm used to seeing from vamps."

"What can I say," I say with a shrug. "I'm an innovator."

A couple of the other hunter's chuckle, and Jackson offers me a hand getting to my feet.

I pry some wet cash out of my wallet and pay for a cab to take the kids to the emergency room. They're both starting to come around as I'm telling the cab driver where to go.

"Who are you?" the blond kid asks, squinting at me blearily.

"Guardian angel," I say offhand. "And hey. No more drinking till you're twenty-one or I'm going to come back and kick your ass."

The kid's eyes widen and I'm afraid he may have taken that a bit more seriously than I meant it.

As the cab takes off, Arsen jogs back across the street from a gas station convenience store with a couple of small hand towels.

"It's all they had," he says, handing me one. "Unless you're interested in a novelty T-shirt with a cat dressed as a taco on it."

"This'll be fine," I agree, ringing out my hair.

"So, now Niko knows we're in town," Jackson begins, sidling up to us. "Does that fuck our plan?"

"No," I say, shaking my head as I try to pat as much excess

moisture out of my clothes as I can manage. The river water stinks like low tide. "It changes nothing. The arrogant fucker already knew we were here."

"How's that?" Jackson asks with a frown, hands on his hips.

"We already paid a visit to his house," Arsen explains, looking away toward the water as he absentmindedly dries himself. "He killed Claudette."

"Rigged her body to explode," I elaborate. "Took the whole place out, burned to the foundations."

Jackson's eyes widen and he pushes a hand through his hair.

"Well, I suppose that's a pretty good indicator of his commitment to this bullshittery," he says. "He's not leaving himself anywhere to retreat to."

"Exactly," I say, frowning as I give up on ever getting dry and toss the towel at a public trash can. "I'm starting to think he wants us to follow him."

Jackson hums a worried note, fingering the belt that holds his knives.

"Oh, that reminds me," I say, and pull out the knife he'd thrown at Niko earlier, offering it back. "These can't be cheap."

"They are not," Jackson agrees emphatically, taking it. Before I can let go of it, he reaches out to catch my hand where it's still on the hilt. He looks at me with grave seriousness in his dark eyes. "Listen. Be careful, all right? If he really is willing to go this far and you think he's pulling you into a trap . . . I know you're tougher than that little son of a bitch by a country mile, but when you get worked up and reckless and stop thinking . . . Just be smart, okay?"

"I promise," I tell Jackson with a crooked smile. "Look at the big bad hunter, worried about a vampire."

Jackson drops my hand and clears his throat, busily putting away his knife.

"Humans have a lot riding on this, too, is all," he lies. "I just don't want you getting yourself killed before this mess is cleaned up."

I chuckle and glance at Arsen, assuming he must be as amused by Jackson's fluster as I am. But Arsen's still distracted, holding his towel in one hand and staring out at the water. I wonder where his thoughts are. Claudette? Niko? The situation in general?

I can see the bruises on his skin from the fall into the river where his wet shirt rides up on his back. He's still got cuts and burns from Niko's house exploding, too. Those haven't healed yet? Jesus, has he been hurting all this time and not told me? I realize guiltily he needs to feed before he can heal.

"I'm beat," I tell Jackson, nodding my head in Arsen's direction subtly. "I'm going to go find a hotel, crash for a few hours."

Jackson quickly picks up on the same thing I have.

"Gotcha," he said. "Me and the boys can take it from here. Get some rest."

I smile at him gratefully, then turn to Arsen, putting a gentle hand on his shoulder. He flinches like a spooked horse, blinking as he returns from being lost in his thoughts.

"Come on," I tell him with a smile. "Let's go find a comfortable bed and some dry clothes. Preferably without any kitschy slogans."

"I don't know," he says, smiling a little as he turns to walk with me. "That taco cat thing was kind of funny."

CHAPTER 12

The hotel room is quiet and dark, a relief after the sweaty, heaving crowds of the street party. I can see Arsen slowing down all the way back. The jump from the bridge took a lot out of him and after everything else, he didn't have a ton of energy to spare. And he's still distracted, caught up in his own thoughts. Anxiety itches at the base of my spine, worrying it's something about me. I shrug it off, pulling the curtains tightly closed and putting out the "Do not disturb" sign as Arsen sinks into an armchair, still wet from the river.

"Hey." I sit down on the edge of the bed facing him and hold out my wrist. He gives me a guilty, conflicted look. I hold it closer to him. "It's all right. You're no good to me all beat up and worn out, remember?"

He doesn't smile, which makes my heart sink down into my stomach, but he takes my arm. I wince at the sting of his teeth and the weird heady rush of blood loss. The distance between us is strange, thick with a weird tension. When we've done this before it's been intimate, romantic. But he almost leans away from me in the chair as he feeds, like he wants to pretend I'm not here, like it's not me he's feeding from. The itch of anxiety grows stronger.

Just as I'm starting to get lightheaded he pulls away, wiping his mouth. I watch the bite marks close up almost at once.

"Arsen," I say quietly. "Are you—"

"I'm going to get in the shower," he says, cutting me off.

He stands up before I can say anything else and I'm so surprised by the brush-off that I can't say anything else until the bathroom door closes between us. I sit on the bed, my stomach in knots, and listen to the shower running. I try to tell myself that it's just the situation, but I can't help fearing I've done something wrong.

My worrying is interrupted by the landline phone on the bedside table ringing. I glance at the clock, confused. It's a couple of hours before sunrise and any vampires we know would have called our cell phones.

"Hello?" I say, picking up the phone.

"You just couldn't stay away, could you sweetheart?"

My mood sours instantly at the sound of Niko's voice. I do not need this right now.

"How the fuck did you get this number?" I ask.

"As though I wouldn't know where you are," Niko says with a small laugh. "I'm your maker, remember? I always know."

That's bullshit and I know its bullshit but it sends a shiver up my spine anyway.

"You killed Claudette," I say, changing the subject.

"Do you honestly care that much?" Niko asks. "If anything, I did you a favor. Now you don't have to worry about Arsen falling back into old habits."

"She didn't deserve that," I reply, hands clenched so tight my nails dig into my palms and the plastic phone creaks. "She was kind of a bitch, but she wasn't evil. She didn't deserve to be used and disposed of like garbage."

"She was garbage, Sasha," Niko says, callously. "Of the worst kind. A person like that should never have been offered immortality. Imagine a world crowded with such vain, vapid, greedy creatures, lacking in all ambition except petty manipulation and base hedonism. Do you really think Claudette, in all of the eternity she was given, could have added anything of value to the world?"

"A person's value isn't determined by what they produce," I say, bristling. "And you're an asshole."

"Oh, please, don't preach to me about the innate value of life." Niko groans. "We're predators, Sasha. That sort of sentiment is hypocritical enough coming from humans."

"Why are you still acting like you have the upper hand here?" I ask, sharply. "Demetri is gone. It's only a matter of time before we catch up to you. You might as well give up now and maybe you'll live to regret this whole stupid coup."

He laughs, loud and harsh, like he's been practicing sounding like a cartoon villain.

"Oh, sweet Sasha," he says at last, sighing. "Do you really think I put all my eggs in one basket?"

My heart stops briefly in my chest. I swallow hard, forcing the panic down. He's baiting me. Bluffing.

"Nothing you can do at this point will make any difference," I tell him, steeling myself. "I have the cure."

"But can you produce it fast enough?" Niko asks, and laughs again as my blood runs cold. He hangs up, and I sit there listening to the dial tone while cold sweat gathers on my skin.

I'm putting the phone back on the hook as Arsen leaves the bathroom, towel around his hips and another drying his hair.

"Did someone call?" he asks.

I nod, my mouth a little dry.

"Niko."

Arsen tenses for a moment, then grins. "Good," he says.

"In what universe is that asshole knowing where we're sleeping a good thing?" I ask.

"Now we don't have to track him down," Arsen says. "The bastard will come to us. And I'll tear him apart."

His smile is savage and sends an odd rush of heat through me. Before I can say anything, the familiar sound of Arsen's ring tone echoes from the bathroom. He hurries to retrieve his cell phone from his pants.

"Is it him again?" I ask, worried. Arsen shakes his head.

"It's a friend from the compound," he replies, and accepts the call. "What's up?"

I can dimly hear the voice on the other end, which greets him with restrained warmth.

"Can you talk? It's about your sister."

I see the instant tension in Arsen's entire body.

"Yeah, hang on," he says hoarsely and takes the phone out onto the balcony, closing the sliding glass door behind him.

I watch him pace the narrow balcony, face pale and lined, waiting nervously for the news. At last he hangs up and comes back inside, sitting down on the edge of the bed, his face in his hands.

"What is it?" I ask nervously.

"It's my sister," he replies, and for a moment I'm certain she's gone. The cure didn't work or the virus had already progressed too far or—But then Arsen drags his hands down his face and I see his smile and the tears of happiness in his eyes. "She's awake. She's going to be fine."

"Arsen, that's amazing!" I shout, forgetting myself for a moment in relief and joy for him. I grab him and kiss him hard in celebration, forgetting the earlier tension. To my delight, he kisses me back. He stands from the bed, picking me up in the process to spin around, laughing against my mouth. I can't stop kissing him, the relief of just that little bit of good news a much-needed balm for all the stupid shit that's been happening lately. His warm mouth devours me, tongue sliding against my own, teeth pressing against my lip. Heat rises in me and his kisses grow slower and more lingering, his hands sliding down to my hips. He pulls my hips against his and I feel him through the thin towel, my pulse jumping and my sex tingling with interest. But as his mouth moves to my throat, I laugh and stop him.

"Wait," I insist. "I still smell like river water. Let me shower first."

He smiles at me, eyes heated.

"Why not both?"

We don't even wait for the water to warm up before he presses me to the shower wall, having stripped off my wet clothes as fast as vampirically possible. He showers kisses and small bites over my throat as cool water rushes over us, rinsing away the evidence of the long, terrible day. Ash and river water swirl away down the drain as he cups my wet breasts, tongue rolling over my nipples, the bare graze of his teeth making them stand flushed and full.

I bite my lip, leaning back against the slick tile, but my impatient hands wander down to his half-hard cock, squeezing just hard enough to hear him inhale sharply, hips thrusting into my slowly stroking hand.

Not one to be outdone, he kisses me again as his warm fingers slip down between my lips, thumb rolling in slow circles over my clit as he strokes my entrance, not quite pressing in, teasing me. I try to choke back my moans, knowing it will make him only work harder to hear them, and stoke him with both hands, teasing his head, tracing the veins, stroking the sensitive frenulum until he shivers, whispering my name against my lips.

He kisses me harder, lips sliding on wet skin and tasting only of clean water. His fingers curling inside me at last, enhancing the pulses of pleasure from my clit at the slow relentless grind of his thumb. He spreads my slick up through my lips, takes my whole vulva in his hand, heel of his palm still rocking against my clit as he squeezes me, spreads my lips, strokes the very edges of my need. Playing with me, exploring, taking note of the things that make me bite back gasps and press into his hands.

"Please," I beg at last, half because I know he loves hearing me beg. "Give it to me."

I half expect him to keep teasing me, but I think he's as desperate as I am. He grabs me under the thighs and lifts. I brace myself against the slick tile wall, grabbing the shower head for stability as he spreads my legs wide and takes a moment just to admire the view, water coursing down my body and my sex wide open, flushed and soft and desperate for him.

"Please," I insist, only partly because I don't know how long I can hold this position.

He doesn't make me wait any longer. I hold my breath as I feel the hot head of his cock against me, sliding through my wet folds, and finally pressing in, slow and easy, aided by the ample lubrication of the shower. I let out a long low groan as he fills me, thick cock spreading me open, sending shivers of pleasure through my entire body. It's easy to underestimate how good he feels inside me any time we're not fucking. When I'm clearheaded I always seem to think there's no way it could possibly feel that good. But God it does.

One hand grips my ass, holding me up, taking some of the strain off my taut thighs squeezing his waist. His other hand supports my hip and keeps a thumb on my clit. As he begins to move, he strokes me in time with his thrusts, slow and deep at first, then faster, harder, as pleasure builds rapidly within both of us. The slap of wet skin echoes in the tile bathroom. Water sluices down our bodies and runs over the place where we're joined, adding another layer of stimulation. My back hurts from pressing into the wall and my arms and legs are shaking with the strain and I don't care. The discomfort just adds to the edge of my desperate need to come. To feel him come.

"Sasha," he growls, ramming me harder, deeper, my skin

squeaking against the tile as every thrust shakes my entire body. He's close.

"Inside," I tell him, my voice husky with need. It's an order, not a request, punctuated by my legs tightening around him. He groans, his hands squeezing me tight, trying to hold off just a little longer. I feel him pulse within me and I bite my lip in anticipation, squeezing around him. He chokes out a curse and buries himself within me as deeply as he can. I feel the warm rush, the additional little bit of fullness as every crevice within me not filled by his cock is flooded with seed. It's a sensation that makes me shake with pleasure. He keeps going, fucking me through his own orgasm, rubbing my clit fast and hard, until the pleasure overwhelms me and I cry out, walls rippling around his cock as every muscle in my body tenses and then relaxes at once. Pleasure floods through me, my vision blanking for a moment.

Slowly, he pulls out, cock dripping, and sets me down on my shaking legs. I release my white-knuckle grip on the shower head, which is bent and may never be the same, and lean against the wall to catch my breath. Arsen kisses me, slow and gentle, not demanding anything. But then he chuckles and my breath catches as his fingers explore my sex again, feeling the wetness of his own seed. He spreads my lips to appreciate the sight of his cum dripping from me for a moment, then rubs it into my lips, spreading it messily over me. His cum-slick fingers graze my oversensitive clit and I shiver, excitement already stirring in my belly again.

"Looks like you still have some cleaning up to do," he says with a grin, fingers pressing into me. "We might be in here a while."

And what kind of idiot would I be if I said no to an offer like that?

Eventually, clean and deliciously expended, we fall naked into bed, legs tangled, skin to skin. It should be an incredibly restful sleep. But dreams find me, even curled up against Arsen's chest.

It's vague, just ever-shifting glimpses. An apple orchard, trees stretching as far as the eye can see, but every apple I pick is full of worms. Rats fleeing a plague ship, carrying the disease with them, one for every house in the city. A man on fire, stumbling into a crowd, lighting the clothes of everyone around him, who panic and flail, spreading gas, flinging napalm, until the fire has spread to the entire crowd and keeps going, filling the air with screams and the smell of burning meat.

I wake, shaking with horror from the images still lingering in my vision, and it wakes Arsen, who looks around for danger, then holds me close, blinking in confusion, until I stop hyperventilating long enough to speak.

"He's going to infect everyone," I say, the truth rising out of the weird metaphor of my dream like a monster out of the mist. "Niko is going to spread the virus to every human on Earth."

CHAPTER 13

Around sunset, we pull up to an old shotgun house on the outskirts of Seattle. It's an old residential neighborhood, rundown and neglected despite its historic significance. Some of these houses probably date back to not long after the city's founding in the 1850s. It's humid but not hot, somewhere uncomfortable on the edge of rain. Washington, as a state, is one of the greenest places I've ever seen. It all feels thick with life the minute you get clear of the urban density.

An older woman with straw-colored hair leans on the porch railing, smoking, when we pull up, and stubs out her cigarette to slip back inside. By the time we climb out of the car, squinting at the fading red sun, Jackson hurries down the front steps to greet us.

"You made it here in good time," he says, patting Arsen's good shoulder. I'm surprised how much their relationship has improved over the time we've been working together. They're almost friends now or at least respectful. "How's the injury?"

"Almost healed up," Arsen assures him. "Nothing to worry about."

"Everyone's set up inside," Jackson says, ushering us toward the house, glancing up and down the street in search of anyone watching. "Things are a bit . . . tense."

"The other coven leaders already here?" I ask, looking at the other cars parked on the street in front of the house. Plain black vehicles that, while not ostentatious, are still obviously new model luxuries. At least they tried to be discreet. Jackson nods, jaw tight. He can't be having a great evening wrangling a bunch of fussy vampire aristocrats in the same house with a loosely allied band of professional vampire hunters.

We head inside and I'm caught off guard the minute we walk through the door. It looks like the NSA is camped out in the dated 70s living room. There's a series of folding tables set up against one wall with three computers. Three of Jackson's people work there, looking over surveillance footage, conversation transcripts, and complicated data I can't determine the purpose of. One person sits in an old wingback that probably came with the house next to the old landline phone, which rings off the hook every time they set it down. They're also juggling a handful of burner cells, relaying whatever information they're receiving to the people at the computers. Several more people crowd around the coffee table, where a map has been spread out, heavily marked in red.

The only vampires in the room, representatives from Istria and Kresova, stand off to one corner, looking sour. Most of the hunters do their best to ignore them. But more than a few cast undisguised dirty looks in the vampire's direction.

There are two groups, an entourage of four or five from each coven, keeping their distance from each other as well as the hunters. I sigh. This mistrust is going to make things difficult. The covens have never worked well together, let alone with hunters.

But as we enter and it becomes clear things are getting started, Jackson shepherds us and some of his hunters toward the dining room. The coven vamps reluctantly follow. For a moment,

I think this all might fall apart over a seating dispute when a hunter and a Kresova vamp lock eyes over the chair nearest the door, but Jackson smoothly gets between them before anything can happen, shooing the hunter off to a spot near the window. Once we're all settled he begins, introducing the other vampires first as Lady Ghenna of the Istria and Duke Orsino of the Kresova.

"And, of course, you know Arsen and Sasha." He greets us with a nod for the benefit of the assembled. "You remember Rhett." He indicates the skinny Louisiana hunter we'd met when we chased Niko out of the street part. "He knows most of the hunters and the vampire activity out of the South and the Gulf Coast. Minnie here manages the Midwest." He gestures to the blond woman we'd seen on the porch when we pulled up. She's probably in her late forties, brown limbs corded with lean muscle, face lined with an excess of worries. A scar curves up from her lip toward her nose. She dresses in worn leather and eyes everyone at the table with equal suspicion. I'm simultaneously wary of her and kind of want to be her. She looks like she could kick the ass of anyone at this table and come back for seconds. "Zoe is representing the East Coast and our support division."

He gestures finally to a young black woman sitting near Minnie, who I almost missed entirely. She's extremely petite, probably only 5'5" counting the poof of her high, natural ponytail. She's squinting at an iPhone through the thin silver frames of her glasses and laughs a little at Jackson's introduction without looking up.

"I mean, it's a bit disingenuous to call us a division just yet," she says, still scrolling through something on her phone. "We're more like a bunch of disparate sidekicks who've just finally started networking."

"Every hunter needs somebody handling the back end of things," Jackson explains. "Tracking down sightings, handling supplies and finances, organizing surveillance—"

"And managing territorial disputes," Zoe interrupts, eyes still on her phone. "I swear that's half the job. There's always some big dick hunter deciding he's got the entire PNW handled on his own and giving himself a hernia because someone dared to track a wendigo across his turf."

"Amateurs," Minnie growls. "Dumbasses like that never last."

"Which is why it's a good thing y'all are finally organizing," Jackson put in. "Having a more solid structure of contacts will do all a lot of good. It'll make things safer for you all as well." He nods to me and Arsen, then the other coven leaders. "Since we'll be able to put the word out about who doesn't belong on the hit list and keep a lid on any newbie hunters trying to kill anything nonhuman he comes across."

"Same thing for our side," I agree. "When new vamps decide to act stupid, you can capture instead of kill, turn them over to us, and let us handle our own."

"If they've killed humans, I'm not capturing shit," Minnie says with cold finality.

"I'm just saying," I try to stay diplomatic, knowing what she's probably seen in her career and that I myself wouldn't be so keen to forgive murder not that long ago. "We've both got inexperienced idiots endangering themselves. It's part of the territory for all of us. Working together we can make sure a lot less of those idiots end up dead."

"It's something to debate later," Jackson says. "Once Niko and the virus are dealt with."

"If this alliance lasts that long," Duke Orsino states. "No one asked us if we wanted to team up with a group of vigilantes who've made a profession out of murdering us."

"You're here, aren't you?" Arsen asks, sharply.

"For the sake of protecting my coven and our race from the virus," he replies, voice icy. "I have no intention of working with these butchers any longer than absolutely necessary."

"Same to you, mosquito," Minnie adds, her stare like steel.

"That's enough," Jackson says loudly. "We'll worry about all that once the virus is dealt with. It's a danger to everyone. If we can't put aside our shit to deal with it, it's going to destroy us."

The table falls silent, like scolded children. Jackson sighs.

"Zoe," he turns to the young woman again. "Give everyone the breakdown."

Zoe finally puts away her phone and reaches beside her seat, pulling out the map they were looking at in the other room and rolling it out on the table.

"This is a satellite map of the US," she explains. "We've had reports of isolated breakouts of the virus in Europe and Asia, but this appears to be where Niko is starting his plague. The red marks are confirmed outbreaks among vampire populations. The blue are infected human populations."

I felt a flutter of true fear looking at the map. The East Coast already crawled with red, and there were blue points all over the map, clustered around population centers.

"As you can see, it's already got a pretty decent reach," Zoe continues. "It transmits like any virus and through vampire bites. A vamp gets infected, bites a few more people before he becomes symptomatic, anyone he bit and didn't kill is now infected as well. And once the vamp succumbs to the virus and turns feral, he'll be biting anything that holds still long enough, greatly increasing spread of infection. Starting in the East Coast was unlucky for us as well. This area is a hub for travel. Once it got into the airports here, it started popping up everywhere."

"Have the humans started noticing yet?" I ask. "Honestly, the CDC could do a lot to slow this thing down."

"They're starting to pick up on it," Zoe confirmed. "The virus isn't usually fatal to humans—it presents with mild flu-like symptoms—but it can be deadly to anyone with a weakened immune system. We're seeing humans with elevated risk factors . . . infants, elderly, people with autoimmune disorders, people recovering from surgery . . .dropping like flies in the areas with high-infected density. But it doesn't respond to the usual flu treatments and with how mild it is in people who aren't immune-compromised, the CDC response is likely to move pretty slowly. Now, that could be fine. The virus dies off on its own in healthy humans after three to four weeks. There's an unusually high rate of reinfection, but with time and CDC intervention it could be wiped out in a couple of years. The only problem is—"

"Niko plans to spread it deliberately," I finish for her, my mouth a grim line.

"Exactly," Zoe confirms. "So our plan has three factors. One, getting the vampire population into quarantine, since feral infected vamps are the most dangerous and unpredictable disease vector. Two, getting the CDC to move faster on recognizing the virus as a potentially dangerous epidemic so we can slow the spread among the humans as much as possible. And three, preventing Niko from intentionally seeding the infection."

"And Jackson and Sasha will be making a good amount of the antidote for any vamps infected," Arsen says. "We don't have a vaccine yet, but at least we can prevent people from turning feral."

The coven leaders frown at him, casting disbelieving glances in my and Jackson's direction.

"Do you really expect us to accept any medicine given to us by a human hunter and Niko's own spawn?" one of them asks.

"They're trustworthy," Arsen tries to insist, but they look unconvinced. "Sasha's been helping us fight the virus from the beginning. And without Jackson, we wouldn't have any of the hunters' support."

The look on the vampires' faces makes it clear they think they would be better off without either. Arsen breathes out through his nose in an impatient huff.

"Fine," he says. "I can't force help on you. If any of your own end up infected, you'll have to deal with it on your own."

They look slightly uneasy at that but don't back down.

"Anyway, Draugur is already in lockdown," Arsen reports. "But we weren't prepared for a siege. We're going to need a steady supply of clean blood soon or we won't be able to hold the quarantine."

"We're secure as well," Orsino confirms. "Our vampires will be safe until this can be dealt with."

"We are also quarantined," Lady Ghenna of the Istria says, speaking for the first time and folding her hands on the table. "And we have a safe supply of blood that should hold us over indefinitely."

"How?" Minnie asks suspiciously.

I have a horrible idea that I know exactly how and I try to gesture to Jackson to stop them but he's too slow on the uptake.

"Several of our court maintain private reserves of live humans," Ghenna replies casually. "Artisanal blood is a fad at the moment. Their health is rigorously monitored, of course."

"You *keep* humans?" Minnie stands up, her hands flat on the table and rage in her eyes.

"Oh, don't get so worked up," the vampire says, condescension dripping from her tone. "They're very happy. All their needs are looked after. I myself have a small free-range herd living on a vineyard in northern California."

Minnie starts to lunge across the table and Jackson and Rhett both grab her to stop her.

"You expect me to cooperate with someone who keeps human beings like farm animals?" she snarls at Jackson, who glances briefly at me. I can tell he's tempted to let go. Hell, I'm tempted to stake the bitch myself. Even if the whole idea wasn't repulsive, bringing it up here clearly shows she's an asshole with no sense.

"The farm will be shut down," I say loudly, and Minnie stops struggling, while Lady Ghenna gives me a wide-eyed look at my presumption. "As will any others. The minute the virus is dealt with."

"And how exactly do you think you are going to enforce that?"

she says with frosty irritation. "You are not my queen. You are not even of my clan."

"You'll agree to shut them down," I say, staring her directly in the eye. "Because otherwise you won't be receiving any assistance from us protecting them. Where do you think Niko will go first when he starts spreading the infection? Are you completely certain he doesn't know the locations of those farms?"

I can tell by the look on her face that she doesn't.

"I will not help protect some vampire's blood farm!" Minnie says.

"Then you condemn those people to death," I tell her. "If the farms can't be protected, then once Niko infects them, they'll be culled. More likely, the vampires will order them harvested immediately and the blood stored to wait the virus out. Or, you can put your big girl panties on, get the fuck over it, and help me ensure they all get released safely when this is over."

Minnie glares daggers at me, but she sits down. All the humans at the table look faintly nauseous at what they're agreeing to, and I feel a bit queasy myself. But we don't have another choice.

"I'll talk to some of my contacts about getting some donated blood sent to the Draugur and the Kresova," Zoe says after a lengthy, tense pause. "In case this takes longer than anticipated. We're already working on the CDC. We've identified some bacterial markers that can be used to distinguish the virus from a mundane flu. If we can get them to start testing for it, they'll notice how widespread it is and start moving to slow it down. Which just leaves Niko."

"He wants to infect the entire human population," I say, leaning over the map. "But he's going to start with humans closest to the covens' compounds. We're his primary target."

"And who will he target first?" Zoe asks.

"Draugur," Arsen and I say at the same time.

"He's a petty bitch and this is at least half personal for him,"

Arsen elaborates. "There are Draugur compounds are here, here, and here." Zoe offers him a marker and he circles them on the map. "You can see how close the initial infection was to this one. Practically in their backyard. He'll hit the largest population centers near these first, I can guarantee it."

"All right, so we split up," Jackson says. "The hunters will keep searching the East Coast, keeping an eye on this compound while controlling ferals coming out of the infected zones. Your group can head west, so the second Zoe's surveillance team catches wind of Niko, there will be someone close enough to nab him no matter where he strikes first."

"What about the cure?" Rhett asks, looking down at all the red marks on the map with a frown. "Or the vaccine or whatever? Jackson said you were close."

"There's not enough time," I tell him, hating to admit it. "If Niko manages to spread it to everyone, any cure will come too late."

CHAPTER 14

We don't linger once the decisions are made, heading out to catch a plane. Jackson stays behind, promising to catch up with us once he's done organizing the hunters, including a few groups to patrol the Istria's blood farms. I have a feeling the Kresova have a few of those, too, (I wouldn't be surprised if the Draugur have a few, honestly) but I can't risk the alliance by forcing anyone to come forward about them right now. Fingers crossed I'll be able to keep my promise to Minnie and get them shut down when all this is over. It seems like a long shot. Even if I do stop Niko and make a vaccine for the virus and single-handedly save the entire vampire race. If history has taught me anything, it's that once a group of people start treating another group of people like things, it's really damn hard to change their minds.

I keep worrying about it as we board the plane. Arsen has his own worries. He's on his phone all the way to the airport and back on it the minute we hit cruising altitude. Talking to the Draugur mostly, organizing the quarantine and the rationing of their supplies, including the remaining doses of the treatment for the virus. It's got a pretty fantastic rate of effectiveness for how fast I threw the thing together, honestly. But no treatment is one hundred percent effective. We're still losing people. And will continue to do so until I can finish a vaccine that will keep people from becoming infected in the first place.

I watch Arsen pace the plane, arguing with one of his officers about sending men to join Jackson's search parties and the patrols for the blood farms.

"Yeah, I hate it, too," he growls, "but if we haven't eliminated the virus before our supplies run out, we may have to rely on the Istria for blood. The only alternative is breaking the quarantine and risking us all to infection again. We've already lost enough people."

I love the authority in his voice, the calm and methodical way he lays out plans and gives orders. He's grown a lot from the man I first met, who relied on his strength to maintain control and only thought about advancing his own power.

"The vaccine will be finished once Niko is no longer a threat," Arsen tells the person on the other end. "Sasha can handle it. No. No, that's not a risk. Sasha can handle herself, too."

He smiles briefly in my direction and I smile back, my heart warming. More important than any other growth, he's learned to respect my strength and my need for space. This will make our relationship last. He trusts me. I trust him.

The plane lands too close to sunrise for comfort and we find a hotel. I drop into bed to sleep. It's been too long since I had any blood and all of this has been exhausting on multiple levels. Arsen kisses me on the cheek.

"I'm running out for a bit," he whispers.

"No, stay," I grumble, trying to drag him into bed. He laughs under his breath and kisses me again but pulls away.

"I've got a few things to take care of first," he says, raising his phone to indicate it's more Draugur business. "I'll be back as quick as I can."

"Be careful," I mumble, half asleep. "Sun's coming up."

"I will."

I'm asleep before the door even shuts behind him.

I wake up to the smell of bacon.

"Room service?" I slur, my eyes not even open yet. I hear Arsen laugh.

"Yeah, I figured we could use a treat."

I sit up, yawning and rubbing my eyes, and he sits down beside me with the tray. The light leaking through the drawn curtains is still pale and watery. I've only been asleep a couple of hours. Arsen and I are both still dressed. I didn't bother to change before falling into bed and I don't think he's laid down yet. But my attention is quickly captivated by the breakfast spread. Bacon, eggs, waffles, muffins, fresh fruit, and yogurt.

"Is that champagne?" I ask, raising an eyebrow as he skillfully fills two crystal champagne flutes with prosecco and orange juice. The stems are decorated with golden ribbons, which seems a bit much to me.

"Like I said," he says with a little smile. "We needed a treat. Everything we've gone through lately . . ."

He hesitates, still holding both glasses, and frowns down at them for a moment.

"I could have lost you," he says. "More than once. I haven't felt that kind of fear since I was human. When you're immortal, it's easy to forget how fast things can change. You get comfortable, thinking you'll live forever, and instead death just sneaks up on you. I don't want to . . ."

He pauses, flustered, his face a little red. I stop picking at the bacon, sensing something is up. He gathers himself, trying to find the words.

"I don't want to miss the chance to appreciate this," he finally says, setting aside one of the glasses to take my hand. "I don't want to take this for granted and risk losing it before I can really show you how I feel. I . . . I want to build a life with you, Sasha. And even if this all goes wrong and we don't get the chance, I need you to know that I wanted that. You mean more to me than anyone ever has."

He presses the champagne flute into my hand and I'm confused for a moment what that has to do with this incredibly touching declaration. Then I feel something hard against my palm, clinking against the crystal stem of the glass.

"Immortality has been worth it because I lived long enough to find you," he says, voice straining with sincerity as I stare down at the champagne flute and the beautiful diamond ring tied to the stem by the ribbon. "Sasha, will you marry me?"

I drop the glass, spilling mimosa all over the sheets, and throw my arms around him, kissing him hard and breathless. He kisses me back, tender and earnest, his hands squeezing my waist. I might go on kissing him until we lose our senses and make love in the champagne-soaked bed, but we hear the breakfast tray slipping and break the kiss to grab it before it can crash to the floor. He laughs as he sets it aside on the night stand and gives me a hopeful, nervous glance.

"Can I take that as a yes?"

"Yes," I say, laughing, happy to feel foolish about this. "Absolutely, yes."

We lie in bed, eating breakfast, ignoring the wet champagne spot, losing ourselves in kisses. I can't stop staring at the ring, which I put on the minute I untie it from the champagne glass.

"It's only temporary," he says, seeing me staring at it again. He takes my hand and kisses my finger right beneath the ring. "I went out to pick something up this morning because I didn't want to wait. But I have one back home, a family heirloom. A real star sapphire, set in silver. I'd like to have it resized for you. It's much nicer and older than I am, which is saying something."

"I don't know," I say with a giggle, admiring the thin white gold band on my finger, its small diamond glittering. "I'm pretty happy with this one."

"Well, I'm not," Arsen says with a playful growl, pulling me closer to drop kisses down my throat and chest. "You deserve better. You deserve the best. You deserve the whole damn world."

Flustered and delighted I don't contradict him.

The phone rings. It's the landline hotel room phone, and I get an uneasy sense of déjà vu as I pull away from Arsen.

"Maybe it's just room service asking if we need someone to come get the dishes?" Arsen suggests.

Hoping that's all it is, I pick up the phone.

"Good morning, beautiful."

It's not room service.

"What do you want?" I demand, anger flaring. How dare he call now, when I was, for half a minute, genuinely happy?

"The same thing as always, Sasha," Nico says patiently. "For you to stop this pointless rebellion and come home."

"Pointless? You're killing your own kind!"

"For the greater good," Niko says evenly. "When I'm done, there will be no more infighting between vampires. No more pointless centuries of feuding. There will be only the Baetal, and a world firmly under our control. No more hiding in the shadows, no more guilt. No more worrying the humans will eventually nuke us all, or worse, kill us slowly by poisoning the planet. We'll be in control, and with the steady wisdom of immortality, we'll fix everything. It'll be a better world for humans, too, you'll see."

"You're literally planning world domination," I say, disgusted.

"Oh, let it go sweetheart," Niko says impatiently. "Every vampire rebels against their Master when they're young. It's natural. But I don't have time to let this run its course. The plan is moving ahead too quickly. I don't want to risk that you might not survive it. If you give up and come home now, you'll be safe. And you'll be beside me when I remake the world. I could make you a queen."

"I'm not interested," I tell him flatly. "You need to stop deluding yourself and give up. You will lose. You've already lost. Just stop before more people get hurt."

"You don't have any idea what you're talking about," Niko scoffs. "My victory was already assured the moment I discovered the virus. It's changing me, Sasha. Refining me."

"You're infected?" Sympathetic horror flashes through me. I thought he was smarter than that, that he would at least protect himself from the virus.

"I'm becoming what vampires were always meant to be," Niko says with perfect confidence. "I'm more powerful than ever. Faster, sharper, more alert. I want to share this with you, Sasha." His voice shifts, becoming softer, more genuine. "You're mine, Sasha. I made you. Chose you above all others to be with me forever. I love you. I know you love me. Come home. Give yourself to me and I will remake the world in your name. Fear me, love me, obey me, and everything you desire will be yours."

"I desire for you to fuck off," I say, but I can't put as much venom into as I'd like. I'm worried about him. Despite everything, he is my maker. It's a connection I don't even fully understand. But it makes my heart ache at the thought of him, infected, probably dying, and still chasing this stupid plan which is only going to get him and a whole lot of other people killed. I don't love him, I don't think I ever could. But I want to save him, and I don't think I can.

"As you wish," Niko says after a moment. "But I'll be waiting. As soon as you realize your mistake, I'll be here to forgive you. Even if I have to wait forever. Even if I have to kill everyone you've ever cared about to make you return to me. Even if I have to imprison you a hundred years before you relent. I'll still forgive you. And once you finally give your heart to me, I will give you the crown of the world—"

I hang up. I don't need to hear any more. My heart beats hard in my throat, and I scrub at my eyes to stop them from tearing up.

"You, all right?" Arsen asks tentatively, taking my hand and pulling it away from my eyes. I force a smile, and look down at the ring on my finger.

"Yeah," I tell him. "Not even Niko can ruin this for me."

CHAPTER 15

Jackson arrives a few hours later and we welcome him up to the hotel room to make plans and work out the specifics of our search. He spreads the satellite map of the area out on the bed, and we sit around it arguing.

"This water treatment facility is closest to the coven," Arsen says, pointing out a spot on the map that he's marked in green. "It's the most likely place for him to hit."

"Unless he isn't going for the water supply," I remind him. I circle a few spots of my own. "There's an airport, a mall, and a stadium all in range of the compound as well. From what we've seen, the virus is primarily airborne. I don't doubt he could get it into the water, but it would be much easier to aerosolize it and dump it over a crowd."

"Even if he does go after the water," Jackson says, "he may not hit the water treatment plant. There's a ton of filters on that thing. And a lot more of it goes to agriculture than it does to consumption. And as far as we know, the virus doesn't transmit to animals. These cave systems could give him stealth access to the water table if he's willing to climb deep enough, and a vampire is bound to be a hell of a lot more successful at spelunking than a human. Or he might hit the Colorado River."

"I don't think he could contaminate the river in enough quantity to actually spread anything," I say with a frown. "That's a hell of a lot of water to poison. And if he doesn't get the concentration high enough, people won't consume enough of the virus to actually infect them. It might actually boost their immunity."

"Does *he* know any of that?" Arsen asks, frustrated. "He's not the scientist behind this, remember? Sasha killed that guy."

I grimace. "Don't remind me."

"I'm just saying, does he have enough knowledge of water distribution on the West Coast, how viruses work, and shit to know any of that? Or will he just go for the most obvious thing because he's out of his depth?"

I think about it for a moment, then drag the notes of the virus's creator closer to read over again.

"God, this guy's handwriting was terrible," I mutter.

"You're telling me," Arsen says with a snort. "I had to try and cure you reading that mess, remember?"

"Yes, and you did a great job, sweetie," I tell him, leaning over to kiss his cheek. He scowls at my patronizing tone but the kiss cheers him up. Jackson shakes his head, then picks up his cellphone as it buzzes with a text.

"Zoe's located some blood for you and your group," he says, reading the text and responding quickly. "She's got an address where someone will meet you with a couple of coolers full of blood packs. Enough to get you and your team by for a week or so."

"Fantastic," I say, sitting up. "I can go and get it."

"No, I'll get it," Arsen says, sliding off the bed and grabbing his jacket. "I've been in this town before; I know the area better. And you need to stay here and help Jackson figure out what Niko's planning. I'll be right back."

"Be safe," I tell him and pull him down to kiss him, lingering a little longer than necessary.

"I'll text you the address," Jackson tells Arsen when he finally breaks the kiss. Arsen nods gratefully and heads out.

"You two are especially sappy today," Jackson says casually as I watch Arsen go with a little sigh. "I'm guessing by that and the new jewelry you're showing off that he popped the question?"

I blush and clear my throat, fiddling with the engagement ring.

"Earlier this morning," I admit.

"Seems like a bad time for it," Jackson says, a sympathetic look in his eyes as he glances at me briefly. "There's a lot of dying happening."

"That's why it's the perfect time," I counter. "If something happens to either of us, at least we can say we, you know, that it meant something. That for at least a couple of days we were . . ."

I trail off, flustered and unsure how to phrase it, tugging on my own hair in embarrassment and happiness as I remember Arsen's little speech. Jackson just shakes his head.

"Whatever floats your boat. Now, how hard would it be for him to make the virus transmittable by liquid?"

We go back and forth for a while and finally decide it's easier and more likely for him to go airborne. There's a big concert scheduled soon at the stadium, which seems ideal for a viral attack, and unlike the airport, is more likely to concentrate infection here around the Draugur compound, which is what he wants. As we continue working out details, I find my mind wandering back to the conversation with Niko over and over.

"What's on your mind?" Jackson asks, the third time I space out and miss what he said.

"Niko called earlier," I admit. Jackson stiffens.

"He knows where you are?"

"He called our last hotel, too. I'm not sure how he keeps finding us."

"That's not good," Jackson says, uneasy. "Is he in the area?"

"I don't know," I say, shaking my head. "He didn't say. He just tried to convince me to give up and go back to him again. He said the plan is moving fast. He's worried I'll get caught in the crossfire and die and he won't have the chance to murder everyone I love and lock me in a cage for a hundred years until I agree to be his obedient pet again."

"Jeez," Jackson says, leaning away from me. "That guys got some issues."

"Yeah," I agree. "And I'm worried they're getting worse. He said he's infected."

"Really?" Jackson says, intrigued. "Maybe our problem will take care of itself after all."

"I don't know about that," I say warily, leaning back on my hands, the mattress creaking under me. "He said . . . he thinks it's changing him. The virus. He thinks it's making him stronger."

"Sounds more like it's making him delusional to me," Jackson snorts. "We've both seen what that virus can do. It's not making anyone stronger."

"I don't know," I murmur, and reach for the half-empty bottle of champagne, pouring myself another glass. "Viruses aren't my specialty. But the body can change trying to fight them off. Most of the symptoms people experience from illness are from the immune response. Fever from chemicals released by white blood cells, muscle aches as your body pulls out proteins to fight the virus, your throat and sinuses closing off and producing mucus to try to flush out and keep out allergens and germs–"

"None of those things turn you into a super vamp," Jackson says. "They just make you tired and miserable."

"But this is a unique virus," I respond. "Made to attack the vampire immune system, which we know practically nothing about. All my first failed attempts to make a treatment or vaccine tried to treat vampire bodies like human bodies, and it didn't work. Vampires, biologically speaking, are as different from humans as humans are from apes. And that's probably understating it, honestly. Not to mention there's magic involved, so any pretense of a scientific approach is kind of out the window! I'm basically re-inventing medicine from the ground up here. So who knows? Maybe it really could make some vampires stronger!"

I down the champagne like a shot and throw my hands up, at a loss.

"I'm going to call Zoe for you," Jackson says. "She might know a bit about vampire biology. Or know someone who does."

"It's worth a shot," I say with a shrug.

I spend another hour talking with hunters about the medical and anatomical info on vampires they've gathered over the years and call a few coven vamps as well, but I don't get much of anywhere. Vampires aren't susceptible to most human diseases, but we can catch a few, and no one knows why or what the difference is or whether what Niko claims is a viable immune response. It's all basically a big shrug and a resounding maybe. I'm so caught up in it that I almost don't notice the sun going down.

"Hasn't Arsen been out a while?" I ask, concerned. Jackson checks the time and frowns.

"Yeah," he agrees. "Shouldn't have taken this long just for a pick up. Maybe he got stuck in traffic?"

I send him a text, and my worry increases about a hundred-fold when he doesn't reply. I call him, but it just rings and eventually goes to voicemail. My heart is starting to beat too hard, my chest feeling tight and bruised. Jackson is making calls, too, and looking increasingly worried. He hangs up a call suddenly and puts a hand over his face.

"What happened?" I ask, frozen, my voice too quiet for the panic rising inside of me.

"He's been attacked."

CHAPTER 16

Arsen stumbles in a little while later on the arm of a hunter I don't know, who turns out to be the contact Zoe sent to bring him the blood. Arsen never showed, and the hunter started to leave, when he found Arsen slumped over in an alley with a silver knife in his gut.

Arsen looks terrible, weak and barely coherent.

"That knife was in him for a while before I found him," the hunter says as I help him over to the bed, shaking with mixed relief and distress. He's alive, thank God, but seeing him like this is horrible. "A weaker vampire would have died."

He brought up the coolers of blood he was supposed to give Arsen, and we pop open a bag, shoving the straw into Arsen's mouth. He sips weakly, but I can see the color returning to his face.

"Thank you," I say, taking the hunter's hand in my shaking fingers. "You saved his life. I can't thank you enough. Anything you need, ever, let me know."

The intensity of my stare unsettles the hunter a little. I would kill people for this stranger right now, and I guess he can see that in my face. He laughs uneasily, pulling his hand away.

"It's no big deal," he says. "I mean, it's definitely a first for me, saving a vamp rather than killing him, but Rhett says you guys are all right and I trust him. You, too, Jackson."

"Thanks." Jackson's a little miffed at having his trustworthiness rank under Rhett's.

"Did you get a look at who did it?" I ask the hunter, my fear beginning the slow burn into fury. "Any idea at all."

"No, it was over way before I found him," the guy says, shaking his head. "I didn't give up and try to leave till a good hour past when he was supposed to meet me. But it had to have been another vamp. I'm no Sherlock Holmes, but I've seen a few knife wounds. Judging by the angle, whoever it was came up behind him. He would have noticed any human trying that, and no human would have been fast enough to knife him that way, either. Whoever it was probably used that knife hoping it would get blamed on a hunter, break up the alliance."

"In which case, it was brave of you to mention the knife at all," I say.

"Machinations and double-crosses are vampire shit," the hunter says with a shrug. "Hunters have figured out that being straightforward tends to cut right through that Machiavellian bullshit. They count on you being liars and shit communicators and making it all worse. But if you get out in front of it and yell the truth loud enough, it stumps 'em."

"That's a good policy," I say thoughtfully, looking at Arsen lying on the bed. "I'll remember that. After I tear Niko's throat out."

I grab my jacket and storm toward the door.

"Whoa," Jackson steps in front of the door, forcing me to pull up short. "Hold your horses there."

"You're not going to stop me," I say, teeth bared.

"'Course not," Jackson agrees. "I'm going with you. I want a piece of that bastard, too. Just tap the brakes for a minute while I grab my weapons, why don't you?"

I back down, however reluctantly, and he relaxes.

"Good," he says. "Plus, someone's gotta watch your ass if you're going up against Niko. Guy's nuttier than a fruitcake."

"He won't hurt me," I say impatiently, pacing back to Arsen's bedside while Jackson checks his crossbow and straps on his knives. "He's still convinced I'll go back to him."

"From what you were saying earlier, it sounds like the virus has got to his brain," Jackson reminds me. "He may not recognize you for all you know."

He has a point, but I don't like it. I take Arsen's hand and he stares up at me, blurry-eyed, and squeezes.

"Be careful," he whispers. He doesn't try to stop me. He knows I can handle it. I half-expect feeble protests that I let him come with me. He must be in bad shape to not even try. I smile at him. The engagement ring glitters between our joined hands.

"Just heal up fast so you can come and help me," I tell him, and lean down to kiss him.

"I love you," he says, the words soft as his lips against mine.

"I love you, too."

Before I can get any more emotional and lose the edge of my anger, I pull away and shrug my coat on.

"Let's go."

Jackson and I make our way to the address Zoe gave Arsen for the pick-up. It's an industrial neighborhood, not far from the water. I find the alley where it happened without even trying. I can smell Arsen's blood half a mile away. The sight of it splashed over the asphalt makes my stomach twist itself into knots.

I force myself to block it out, testing the air for a different scent. It isn't Niko, but it is something. A splash of darker color near Arsen's blood.

"He hit whoever attacked him," I tell Jackson, kneeling to point out the splash. "Not much, but enough for me to get a scent."

"Lead on, Lassie," Jackson says. "I'll follow you."

I point a threatening finger at him. "Make another hunting dog joke and I'll eat you."

Jackson grins. "Guess it'd be bad idea to call you a bitch, then."

I fake a swing at him and feel a moment of satisfaction when he ducks.

I lead him deeper into the maze of old warehouses and factories, most shut down and abandoned decades ago when shipping moved farther down the coast and production moved overseas. But I'm starting to have trouble keeping the scent, and it's difficult to narrow it down to a point of origin. I'm not a bloodhound.

"There," Jackson says, pointing to a low storage building ahead of us. "The windows are painted over but the structure is collapsing so there won't be any squatters unless they're real desperate. Perfect place for a vampire to lay low."

"Knew I brought you along for a reason," I say, and together we head toward the warehouse, staying out of the moonlight.

We slip in through a side door that's warped so badly it won't fit in the frame. Inside, it's pitch black. I can still see, in the weird flat shades of gray of my vampire night vision, but Jackson is blind, and putting on a light would reveal us to whoever's in here. He grabs the back of my shirt instead as we move silently, deeper into the cavernous room. He knows he can't ask anything or risk revealing us, and I can only imagine how nerve-wracking that must be for him. Especially when I stop abruptly.

"You got a light?" I ask in a bare whisper, as the sound of strange hissing and growling begins ahead of us.

"Cover your eyes," he answers, and chucks a UV grenade into the center of the room. It explodes in a burst of searing white light that dazzles me even with my arm shielding my eyes. It burns the skin off a pack of feral, infected vampires that emerge from the garbage ahead of us. It also pisses them off.

Jackson and I leap into action. He pulls his crossbow, firing by the still-fizzing light of the grenade, which casts everything in stark black-and-white shadow. I take a knife in each hand and focus on keeping the mindless vampires from getting too close to him. I move like somebody taught a blender how to dance ballet, dodging claws and teeth as I slash open throats and bellies. I aim for tendons whenever I can, trying to disable rather than kill. Not that I think these poor assholes can be saved, but when it comes to a vampire, even a disease-ravaged zombie vampire, disabling is a lot easier than killing. I have to keep a cool head, not let myself get lost in the killing, the smell of blood. Staying rational is the only advantage I have over these things.

Jackson keeps backing up, trying to keep the ferals from getting behind him and circling us. There's so goddamn many.

"There!" I shout, pointing behind us at a crane operator's booth. It's got four walls, one solid with a heavy security door, two set with thick industrial plate glass. The front wall has the same glass, but it's been knocked out or removed, leaving a perfect half wall for hunkering down behind. Jackson's grenade is sputtering its last, but he books it by the last of the light to the safety of the booth. I cover his retreat and vault in a second after he lights a flare. He pops back up over the wall a second later with his shotgun, spraying the pursuing ferals with silver birdshot.

"You know," he says as he reloads the shotgun while I knife anything stupid enough to try and get over the wall. "Just because Arsen nearly got himself killed on a milk run doesn't mean you needed to do him one better."

He pops up again, unloading another two barrels of silver shot into the crowd of ferals. It's loud as hell in the empty, echoing warehouse and it leaves my ears ringing.

"What's a relationship if not taking turns putting yourself in mortal peril for each other?" I shoot back, nearly taking off the head of a feral trying to leap over the wall. I kick it back out, knocking over another two in the process. "How much of that silver shot do you have?"

"Few more rounds," Jackson says. "Then it's back to crossbow bolts."

"Better make this fast then," I say, and move out of the way for him to blast another hole in the crowd with the shotgun before I jump out and begin mowing them down with my knives. Their teeth rake me, opening bloody wounds on my arms and legs and I feel a terrible pulse of worry at the thought of catching the virus again. I've had it once, I've had the cure. I should be fine. And even if I'm not, I'm sure as hell going to take as many of these fuckers with me as I can. For what they did to Arsen, I'll kill every one of them.

I taste blood, and rage boils in me. I move faster than I ever have. My vision becomes a series of vulnerable spots, the flash of my knives. I hear nothing but my ears ringing and the heart beats of the ferals. Time slows down and stops existing.

And then, finally, I turn to face the next enemy, and there's no one there. I don't believe it for a moment, whipping around, certain I've missed something, but there's no one there.

"Sasha."

I jerk toward the sound, knives raised, my nerves still on edge, but Jackson holds up his hands to show he's not a threat, though he's still holding the shotgun in one of his hands. My heart races and breathing hurts. I'm drenched in blood, and most of it isn't mine. There's dead ferals two inches deep everywhere Jackson's light reaches.

"You got 'em all," Jackson says, staring at me. His eyes are wide. He almost seems a little scared. "You can relax."

I drop the knives rather than put them away. My fingers hurt from gripping them so tightly.

"You, all right?" I ask Jackson, my voice a little hoarse as I shuffle toward him.

"Yeah, not a scratch on me," he says, still sounding worried. "You?"

"Took a few chunks out of me," I admit. "Nothing that won't heal soon."

"I've never seen anything like that," he says, and I realize where that fear is coming from. It's me. He's scared of me. I must look like a monster. But Jackson shakes it off. He climbs out of the booth and puts a hand on my shoulder. "Hey. I'm a certified badass, all right? Vampire killing machine. But I definitely would have died if you weren't here. So, thanks."

It's pretty awkward as far as thank you's go, but I'll take it.

"Jesus," Jackson says, looking down at all the bodies. "How did we not know there was a nest like this out here? They're all fully gone. Maybe . . . a bunch of covenless infected holed up here? Tried to wait it out? Or lock themselves in so they couldn't hurt anyone else?"

I shake my head.

"No," I say, and I begin looking closer at the bodies, a sinking feeling sending my gut down to my shoes. "Too many. And the doors weren't even sealed. They were brought here from somewhere else."

I kneel, pulling up the sleeve of a dead feral to confirm my suspicions. Jackson hurries to retrieve the flare from the control booth so he can see, too.

"Niko isn't going for the water supply," I say as he comes back. "He's going to unleash a horde of feral."

Jackson leans closer with the flare to see the Baetal tattoo on the dead feral's arm.

"He's turned his own coven into a zombie army."

CHAPTER 17

We pull up to the Seattle coven's compound, and despite myself, I can't stop my jaw from dropping. If I thought Arsen's mini-castle was huge, this is like the Palace of Versailles, the gothic vampire edition.

"Um . . . Arsen? How many vampires are in this coven?" I ask.

He walks around the car, placing his hand at the small of my back. "About five hundred or so, last I checked. Why?"

"Because they're giving royalty a run for their money with this castle of theirs."

Arsen chuckles, tugging me into his side. "Who do you think helped draw up the plans for Louis?"

"Stop it." I blink up at the imposing doors.

"He's just messing with you, Sash." Jackson laughs.

"No, he's not."

I turn toward the newcomer's voice. He's shorter than your average man. Maybe five six or so. His hair is pulled back with a strip of leather, and he's so pale I swear I can see the veins under his skin.

"Sasha, my love, this is Gregor, the master of the Seattle Draugur coven."

Gregor bows low to me and I glance at Arsen, unsure if I should curtsy or something in return. He shrugs and I suppress a growl at his unhelpful gesture, instead thrusting my hand out to Gregor.

"Pleasure to meet you, Gregor."

He stares blankly at my hand, and then grasps it in his, lifting it to his lips and kissing the back. His lips are cool to the touch, and while I appreciate that this gesture is meant to show respect to me, it's still a bit creepy. I guess when you come from the time of Marie Antoinette though, old habits die hard. Or not at all.

"And this is Jackson, the hunter we spoke about." Arsen jumps in, taking my hand in his and entwining our fingers before I can wipe the back of my hand on my pants.

Gregor's eyes narrow as he turns his attention to Jackson. "Ah, yes. Your pet vampire hunter. You'll forgive me if I don't shake your hand for fear of losing it." Gregor's lips form a thin line.

"Hey, no offense taken. It's not like I'm exactly at ease surrounded by vampires, but I'm not here to harm you, I'm here to help you." Jackson's voice is even and calm despite the slight from Gregor.

"If Jackson isn't welcome at the Seattle coven, then you can count me unwelcome as well," I say.

Gregor is the Master in Seattle, sure. But Arsen is the Master of the Draugur of the entire continent. Seeing as how I'm his mate or his consort or whatever it is that we're calling it, I might as well use it to my advantage if only for time's sake.

"Is that so?" a man from behind Gregor growls.

"Yes, it is." I keep my gaze focused on Gregor, not even bothering to address his minion.

"Father, we spoke about this. Let us move on from the posturing and focus on what the true problem is. Nikolai and his maniacal plans. *Oui?*"

Gregor dips his head and steps to the left, revealing the girl the melodic voice belongs to. "My daughter, Darya."

"Nice to meet you all." She smiles warmly. "Now, let's get inside and discuss how to end that Baetal scum's life, shall we?"

I grin at Jackson. "I think I'm in love with her."

He doesn't even look my way when he mumbles, "You and me both."

I shake my head at his smitten expression. This will probably not end well for my friend, but hey, who am I to cockblock him?

"I wouldn't try it, friend." Arsen claps Jackson on the shoulder as we walk into the fortress. "She's what you'd call off fucking limits."

Jackson scoffs. "Relax. It's not like I'm going to go hump her leg or something. I'm here on business. Not pleasure."

"So many jokes, so little time," I mumble to lighten the mood.

"Say one word about my stake, and I'll throat-punch you, Sash."

"Rude, Jackson. I'm on your side." I feign a punch to his side.

Jackson ruffles my hair and when a throat clears, we both separate from our tussle with matching expressions of chagrin.

"Sorry, we grew up together. He's like my annoying older brother."

"Interesting," Gregor remarks, before turning to the room of vampires, all eyeing us with blatant shock. "This is Arsen Eskandar, his mate, Sasha, and their friend, Jackson. I'm sure some of you have heard of Jackson's vampire hunting ties, but he's here to help us stop the Baetal from infecting all of us, so please don't make his stay here too rough."

"We don't need help from his kind!" someone shouts from the back of the room, and I raise a brow.

"Oy, step forward and say that to our faces." No one steps forward and I nod. "Yeah, I thought so. Without Jackson's help, I wouldn't have found the cure in time to save not only myself, but the rest of Arsen's coven in Portland, and the others Nikolai tried to infect in Boston and on the East Coast. So pipe down."

Darya snorts, covering her face with her hand as she tries to hold back her laughter. "You and I are going to get along famously, Sasha."

I smile at her. "I had a feeling we might." I rub my hands together. "So where can we set up so we can talk strategy on stopping Nikolai from attacking you guys?"

"Right this way." Darya holds her arm open, leading us down a hall to a conference room of sorts.

"That will be all, Darya. We can handle it from here," Gregor orders.

"Father, I am an asset to this team."

"You aren't a warrior, daughter. Do as I say. Now." He turns his back to her and I watch as rejection, sadness, and then anger roll over Darya's soft features.

"Of course, Father." Darya leaves, the door a soft click behind her.

I lean over to Arsen, resting my hand on his thigh. "What the hell was that about?"

"She's not meant to be a warrior. From what I understand, Gregor plans to arrange a match for her to strengthen his alliances with other covens."

"And that doesn't concern us?" I ask.

"Not at all. It's a common practice. He will probably make a match with a coven in Europe, so I'm not concerned."

"And if that's not what she wants? What then?"

"I am sure she could go out on her own, or find another coven, but most other leaders won't go against Gregor. After me, he's one of the most powerful vampires in Northern America."

"You guys really need to update your rules of what is and isn't okay these days. Arranged marriages are something that they report on the news, not something that is acceptable among civilized cultures."

Arsen chuckles, kissing at my neck. "Who said we were civilized, love?"

Desire trickles through me, warming my center and I inhale a deep breath, trying to calm my raging libido. "Certainly not you."

More vampires shuffle in, a few of them carrying notebooks and hopeful expressions, a few others with open looks of hatred and anger on their faces as they stare at Jackson. I lean back in my seat, thankful that I don't get headaches anymore, because by the looks of these vampires, I'm about to have one hell of a migraine.

~

Four hours later, I'm standing behind my chair, furious and riled up form arguing with each and every vampire other than Arsen in the room. Jackson is shouting at one vampire who's been a real asshole to both of us, telling him where he can shove his ideas, when I snap.

I hold two fingers to my lips and whistle loudly, startling everyone. "Everyone sit the hell down and shut the fuck up." They all stare at me with mouths wide open in shock and I growl. "Don't make me say it a second time."

Asses hit chairs and I take my time to meet the gaze of every single one of them before speaking.

"I'm only going to say this once, so don't just hear me, listen to me." I cut a glance to a vampire as he opens his mouth, but at my stare, he shuts it just as quickly with a clack of his teeth.

"We are not here to discuss vampire politics and how to go against the vampire hunters. Jackson isn't here to hurt you or your families. So forget about the fact that he's a vampire hunter. It's not relevant right now. His allies are helping to save you from one of your own."

I circle around the table, unable to stand still. "He helped create the cure that will save you should Nikolai sneak past your defenses."

I hold up a hand to stop any arguments before they can even get defensive. "I'm not saying they're not incredible. I'm not even saying we're here to help you defend your compound. I'm saying we're here to catch Nikolai before he can infect any of your thralls, any of your vampires, anyone that could come in contact with you and leave you all dead. As in no longer living. Not just undead, but straight up cold in the ground, and not in the way that you did in the old days. So shove your prejudices up your asses and focus. For the love of fucking God."

"Are you done?" Gregor asks.

"I don't know." I address the room. "Am I? Is my point made? We all clear on what's going to happen next?" They all nod, and I smile at Gregor. "Yes, I'm all set."

Shortly after that, we leave the room, a plan to corner Nikolai in place. I lean my head on Arsen's shoulder, exhausted from arguing with stubborn vampires older than the United States.

"I think I need some air." I rest my chin on his arm, looking up into his blue eyes.

"Then let's go for a walk." Arsen asks Jackson, "You going to be okay by yourself?"

"Yeah, I think I'm okay. I wanted to chat with one of their security guys about how he can make their protocols more secure anyways."

I shake my head. "You're crazy. We just argued with them for hours, but you want more."

Jackson shrugs, walking backward. "What can I say? I'm a glutton for punishment."

Arsen and I walk down to the gardens at the back of the house, and I run my hands over the impressive array of flowers and sculpted shrubbery. I listen to the sounds of the night around us—birds settling down for the night, bunnies scurrying across the back half of the yard, headed to safety, and the faint sound of the city in the background.

"I wasn't expecting it to be so hard to get them to listen to us back there."

"What did you think they would say when we told them we wanted to discuss all their security protocols with a vampire hunter in the room? Here are the blueprints, go nuts?"

I bite my lip. "Um, yes. You're the master over all of the covens. I assumed they wouldn't say no to you."

"You know it doesn't work that way. Or at least, I don't enforce it. I am only one vampire. And now that we're spread out over such a large area, I can't patrol everyone as easily as I could."

"So you're telling me you're like a powerless figurehead?" I scratch my head, thoroughly confused. This was nothing like what I read during the Provokar.

"Not at all. I'm very much the ruler. It's just complicated."

"Of course it is. Nothing is simple around here. That would make things boring."

"Uh oh. Can't have you bored. You might leave me for someone else." Arsen jokes, turning me so I'm facing him, his arms wrapped around me.

"I think I tried that once. And it didn't really work out for me." I'd been miserable. Cranky, duped by a psychotic vampire or two, and let's not forget the whole, almost killed by a deadly vampire parasite.

Arsen leans down, his lips brushing mine softly. "Didn't work out? Are you sure?" He eliminates the inch of space left between us until we're pressed so close together, I can feel each inhale of breath he takes against my chest.

"You're right. It totally worked out. I've got you. And I've got Jackson. And I'm not sick. And we're going to stop the bad guy. It's like a fairy tale." I trace a finger down his jaw.

"Hate to interrupt, princess, but we just found a poison apple, and you've got to come save the damsel." Jackson's voice rings out through the quiet night behind us, and I glance over my shoulder at him.

"I wish you were kidding. But I know you're not. What's happened now?"

"Nikolai is on the phone. He's demanding to speak to you and only you."

"Did he say what he wants?" I ask, praying that he won't make me drag every detail out of him like he normally does.

"Yeah, he's got Darya, and if you don't deliver yourself to him in the next hour, he's going to give her a new mutation of the parasite that he claims our cure won't work on."

"Of course he does." I kiss Arsen, full on the lips, letting my tongue drag across his mouth. "Time to go save the day again, babe."

CHAPTER 18

I walk inside the compound, rage rushing through my veins that Nikolai somehow got his hands on someone I have to sacrifice myself for. I reach for the phone Jackson picks up from a side table, ignoring the group of vampires huddled around anxiously.

"Jackson, give me the phone." I growl when he holds it away from me.

"Stay calm, Sash. He's got Darya, so you can't lose your cool. I know you hate his guts and want to spread them on the pavement like a bunch of cherry jam but stay collected."

I take a deep breath, and then another, grasping for calm. "Thanks. I'm good." I take the phone he hands me and decide to play into Nikolai's delusions. "Niko, my love, I hear you're looking for me?"

"Ah, Sasha. I've missed your sweet voice." He sighs into my ear and I try not to gag in revulsion.

"I've missed you, too, Niko. Jackson told me you're threatening a friend of mine. That's not very nice. Why do you want to hurt me?" I play stupid, hoping that he'll give me something. Slip up and get sloppy.

"You left me no other choice. You're with that Draugur slime, and I can't get your attention otherwise."

"Well that's just not true. I've been chasing after you for weeks now, Nikolai." A movement to my left catches my eye and Jackson rolls his hand, telling me to keep him talking. He must be tracing the call with all his fancy hunter tech. "What is it that you want for my friend's freedom, Niko? Tell me and it's yours."

"I want you with me, Sasha."

"Tell me where you are and I'll come to you."

Niko laughs mirthlessly in my ear. "Do you think me a fool? I know that you'll tell them where I am."

"Why would I do that? I want Darya to come home to her family unscathed and not sick, so I'll come to you without backup, without anyone watching. Just name the place, Niko, and I'm there." God am I there. With a stake, a gun or two, perhaps a knife dipped in silver, and a Mack truck to run him over with.

"Sixty-seven fifty-eight North Salem Street. Be here in less than an hour, or your friend gets a syringe full of death." The line goes dead and I look to Jackson.

"Did you get his location?"

Jackson nods. "Yeah, same address he just gave you."

"Excellent, well, I'm going to go get Darya, I'll be right back."

"Sasha—"

"I know, Arsen, I was kidding. I'm not going in there without backup. I'm brave but I'm not idiotic."

Jackson snorts. "Debatable."

I punch him and he winces. "Cram it, doofus. Let's figure this out. We have ten minutes." I spot Gregor in the room. "You and your vamps know the area better than we do. Can you tell us what our best vantage would be?"

"I'll tell you whatever you need so long as you get my daughter back." The stricken vampire is not quite sure how to process that he could lose the daughter he so carelessly tossed aside earlier today. It takes me aback, but I should be used to vampires surprising me at every turn by now.

"Great, let's get a map and get to work."

With twenty minutes to spare, I drive up to the curb of the abandoned warehouse Nikolai is keeping Darya in and get out. I hold open my jacket and show Nikolai that I'm not armed. At least, not in the way he assumes I will be.

I've got a syringe with the cure for the parasite shoved down my bra, a plastic cap on the needle between my boobs and his sanity.

"Nikolai, I'm here. I'm unarmed, and I'm ready to see Darya," I call out as I enter the warehouse. Rats skitter away as I walk inside, their squeaking sending goosebumps over my arms. The air is dank with molds and the odor of diesel and there couldn't be a more disgusting place on the face of the earth. This is where Niko chooses to claim me.

A romantic he isn't.

"Yoo-da-lay-hee-ooh," I yodel. "Niko, I'm here, just as you asked."

"Sasha." His oily voice oozes from a dark corner of the warehouse. "Where are your friends?"

I hold out my hands.

"You said 'alone.' I'm alone. Where is Darya?"

"I'll send a message to Arsen when we're safely away."

"No can do, Niko. I need to see she's okay before I leave with you. That was the deal. You wouldn't break a deal now, would you?"

"Maybe, I will. You've caused me so much trouble."

In a blur I barely follow, Niko jerks my head onto his leather-covered shoulder. Stunned, I can't fight him off before he has an iron grip around me, keeping me mostly immobile.

"Sasha." He draws each sound out slowly, one hand stroking my hair, the other holding me still. "You know, I missed you. I don't think I've ever missed anyone before, but then I have your blood in me, don't I? And you have mine in you. We're joined, irrevocably, married in the most intimate of ways." He licks behind my ear, and I shiver, but in disgust, not pleasure. Niko gives new meaning to the term "batshit crazy."

"Niko, darling," I murmur.

"Yes, Sasha."

"You know I fucking hate you, right?"

"Love. Hate. There is a thin line. For instance, right now I want to suck you dry just to leave you thirsting, unable to die, unable to drink. It's an exquisite form of torture. And you are so delicious. But you know, so much to do, so much virus to distribute, so little time. So, we'll have to delay that little entertainment." The bastard kisses the back of my neck and I want to rip his head off his shoulders. But I keep my cool. Darya's life depends on it.

"You know what?"

"What, little rabbit?" he asks, smugly.

"Tell me where Darya is."

I don't know if it will work. I haven't compelled anyone in a while, and I have no idea if it can work on Niko, especially in his deranged state. But I put every force of my will into the command.

"In my car."

Then Niko gasps and weakens his grip involuntarily "What did you do?" he hisses. "How did you do that?"

"Sweetheart," I say. "There is soooo much more I can do to you. And that's why I came here. Your life, Niko, is over."

"No!" he screams.

Niko shoves me hard and I fly across ten feet of warehouse into the corrugated steel wall, shocking me with the force of it. I stand shakily, fighting to recover my legs. The asshole catches me by surprise. Never for a second do I think Niko will run. But he does, and I take off after him, following his footsteps through the dark warehouse. But Niko is fast, so much faster than me, and a door slams. I tear the door open and see with relief the shiny Porsche sitting outside the door. Jackson stands by it, looking fierce.

"He took off," he says, "down that alley."

"Fuck." I run down the alley, but I can no longer hear his footsteps. Niko's gone. I have fucked everything up, once again.

CHAPTER 19

As it turns out, Niko's people hate him more than I do now. The call is anonymous and lasts less than a minute, so the vampire who tells us the address doesn't have any other information. Other than where another of Niko's safehouses are.

"This could be a trap," says Arsen.

"What else is new," says Jackson.

And with those glum words, we climb into Arsen's car and travel the twenty miles to the river, and another long line of abandoned buildings, this time a defunct army base.

"He sure knows how to live the high life," I say.

"He's going to keep out of sight. You told him you were going to kill him Sasha. You gave him no reason to think otherwise."

"Well, don't send me on secret missions, then," I pout.

"I didn't send you anywhere," says Arsen. "I did not want you to go. But as I've learned, there is no stopping you when you get an idea into your head."

"It's what you love about me. Admit it. It's true. You just think I'm as cute as fuck when I kick ass."

"As long as it's not my ass, yes."

Arsen squeezes my thigh.

"Downshift for me," he says with a smile.

"What?"

"Sasha, we're going around this corner in a minute, downshift so I don't have to move my hand."

I shift the stick, while Arsen reaches between my legs and rubs his fingers on my mound.

"Upshift, darling, or we're going to stall."

"What the fuck?" I gasp as he hits that spot where pleasure spreads through me. "What kind of freaky stuff is this?"

"The good kind," he grins devilishly at me. "I just want to show you what we can accomplish together, what I always think we can accomplish together. Downshift again."

Oh hell, he is driving me crazy, and I fight to keep my mind on the proper shifting while he concentrates on revving my engines. And I swear I will get him back for this, for bringing me to the edge while I shiver with fear that I'll wreck the clutch or that we'll go spinning into a building. I will because I can't hold back as my body trembles with the urge to explode.

Arsen finally moves my hand off the stick and stops the car, pulling to the side of the road before the gates of the base, and I want to scream because I didn't come yet.

"Arsen?" I say in a warning voice. "Are you forgetting something?"

"Am I?"

"You know you are."

"Oh yes," he says thoughtfully. He leans over the stick and kisses me with a passion that makes me want to crawl on top of him, but his hand holds me down, as his other hand strokes me to the peak of pleasure.

"Come, Sasha. Come for me now."

White light explodes in my eyes as his mouth covers my scream. And I cling to him as if he is my life's breath and I can't do anything else but hang onto him.

Finally, my vision returns.

"I love you," whispers Arsen. "And always will."

"I love you."

And I could have stayed there for hours but we can't. We have a vampire to hunt.

We climb and drop down with vampire stealth. Staring at the huge complex, we realize it will take us hours to search.

"What are we going to do?" I ask.

"Call him."

"Just like that?"

"He can't resist you. Call him."

I shake my head and let out a call like I'm trying to find an errant cat.

"Niko," I call. "I'm here for you. You ran away, darling, and I'm crushed."

"I said call him," growls Arsen. "Not make love to him."

"Hey, I'm working with what I got here. Niko!"

A light turns on in a building a quarter mile down the road.

"He heard you," Arsen grumbles.

"Let's go."

We decide I should enter through the front, and Arsen the back, hoping to catch him by surprise.

"Be careful," Arsen says before he crushes his lips to mine.

"You too." Because even though we are working together, we won't be back to back and Niko is a sneaky, underhanded, son of a bitch.

While I'm trying to administer the cure so Niko can be tried for his crimes, I'm not entirely sure I want him to survive. After everything. All the lives he's taken, the ones he's ruined, I'm not sure he deserves it, but even though I'm immortal, I'm no God, and I suppose I'll have to leave his future up to fate.

I round the corner and find Niko curled up in a ball, rocking back and forth, muttering to himself.

"Niko . . ." I whisper his name, trying not to startle him. He doesn't move. I take a few steps forward, and my foot hits a metal tin, sending it skittering across the floor. Niki jumps up and lunges at me, his eyes red, his fangs exposed.

"Niko! It's me, Sasha. Let me give you the cure." I fight him off, pushing at his shoulders and trying to avoid his fangs at the same time. I pull the cap off the syringe with my teeth and plunge it into his neck. It only enrages him further.

"You shouldn't have done that, little rabbit." He growls. And for a moment, I flash back to when he turned me, beaten and bruised on the floor. He'd bitten me and made me what I am.

It's all the time he needs to strike a blow to my cheek and I fly backward into a pile of boxes.

"Fucking hell." I jump up, but he's on top of me, and I struggle against him, trying to get the upper hand. "Arsen! Arsen! A little help over here!" I scream the words, hoping they'll distract Niko, but his nostrils flare and he narrows his gaze on me.

"Mine. You're mine, little rabbit."

"I'm not yours, Niko. Snap out of it. Chill out and let the cure do its job."

"It's too late. You can't cure me."

His words make me go cold, and I still for a fraction of a second, taking in his jittery pulse, the way his eyes are ruby red and bulging. Spittle flies from his mouth, and his skin is so pale, it's translucent.

"What have you done, Niko?"

"Ensured that I'll win."

I kick him off of me, and he flies past Arsen, almost knocking him over. Arsen advances on him, but I shout at him. "Arsen, no. He's mine."

"Did you give him the cure?"

"I tried, but he says there's no hope for him. That I can't cure him." I press my foot down on Niko's neck, and he claws at it with his hands. "I think he's right. These symptoms aren't correct. I think the cure sped up whatever new mutation he gave himself."

"So what do we do? Contain him?"

I shake my head. "It's too risky, Arsen. If he infects anyone else, I'm not sure how it would spread. Or if I could cure this one."

"So there is only one choice." Arsen hands a blade to me, and I take it from him with a nod.

"But first, we need to know where Darya is." I hold the blade to Niko's throat. "Tell us where you put her, Niko, and I'll make it quick."

He laughs, twisting under me and trying to bite the leather of my boot. "You'll never find her."

Arsen's phone beeps, and I nod at him. "Check it." We had left the team to search the area for Darya in hopes she might be there. God, please tell me they found her.

"They've got her. She was tied up a few buildings over." He slides his phone back into his pocket. "End this fucker so we can go home."

Without a second thought, without a sliver of doubt, I draw the blade across Niko's neck, severing his head from his shoulders. His body twitches, and I step away, avoiding the pool of blood spreading out from his body.

Arsen reaches down to grab his head but I stop him. "Don't touch it. We need to burn it to be sure we eliminate whatever virus or parasite or whatever he dosed himself with. I don't want to ever have to deal with this again. Even by accident."

He pulls a lighter out of his pocket. "Okay, then let's do this." He holds the flame to Niko's shirt and waits for it to catch fire before he steps back. We watch as he turns to ash, and I try to find some kernel of regret or sadness inside of me, but I can't.

Call it newfound vampire coldness, call it experience, or call it good riddance, but the threat to me and my loved ones is gone, and hopefully there will be a peace between the Draugur and the Baetal now that Niko is gone.

A few hours later, we're back at our Portland compound, surrounded by Arsen's coven and one hell of a celebration. Champagne flows like water, and so do blood bags. Another of his vampires passes by me with a nod of respect and a "Thank you, my queen," and I frown.

"Arsen, why are they calling me 'Queen'?"

"Because you are."

"They don't call you King though—"

"Because I told them not to. It's an old ritual."

"Well make them stop it. I'm not a queen. I'm barely even a grad student."

Arsen laughs, pulling me into him, and pressing his mouth into mine. Our tongues tangle, and I press my body into his, loving the feel of his hard muscles against my soft curves. "We should take this somewhere else."

"Sasha, are you trying to take advantage of me?" Arsen jokes, feigning shock.

"Yes, yes, I am. Now follow me to my den of iniquity, so I can blow your mind."

"And other things I hope," Arsen quips.

"Ugh, so gross, guys," Jackson grumbles as he steps into our path.

"So get out of the way, so you don't have to hear it." I laugh.

"I'm headed out, but I wanted to say goodbye before I left." Jackson smiles softly at me.

"One second, okay?" I pull my hand from Arsen's and he nods. I step away with Jackson until we're in a quiet corner. "Hey, you don't mean bye forever, right? Just tonight?" His words strike a cord and I can't lose him now. Not after everything we've overcome together.

"Not forever, but for a while. I think we need some space between your coven and my unit."

"What do you mean? We all are getting along just fine." I frown at him in confusion.

"Just because we united to defeat one enemy doesn't mean that thousands of years of family history disappears and our duty to mankind is over, Sash. It doesn't work like that."

"Why can't we make it work, Jackson?"

"Because you're the queen of the Draugur vampires, and I'm the leader of a vampire hunting faction. We're natural enemies."

"No, you're a natural jackass, but we're not enemies. I refuse to accept that." I cross my arms across my chest.

"And what if one of your vampires attacks a human? What then, Sash?" Jackson grabs my hand in his. "Do you think I want to lose my best friend? I don't. But I don't see how this could work long-term."

"If any of my vampires go after a human, I'll help you hunt them down. Simple as that. There is no reason to do it anymore. We have blood banks for a reason." I wave my hand. "What next? I'll tell you how we get around all of this."

"Sasha—"

"Don't you, Sasha, me. What about Darya? What if you get the call to hunt her down one day? Will you kill her, Jackson?"

He scowls at me. "That's a low blow, Sasha."

"Hey, I'm just keeping it real. I'm not about to lose my best friend over some outdated bullshit."

Jackson laughs. "God, you're not going to leave me alone until I give in, are you?"

I lean forward and hug him, squeezing just a little harder than normal. "Did you forget?" I spin around in a grand gesture, finally feeling like I've come into my own. "I'm mother-fucking immortal. I'm not going anywhere."

WANT MORE VAMPIRES? KEEP READING FOR A SNEAK PEEK AT AURORA: THE KRESOVA VAMPIRE HAREMS VOLUME ONE!

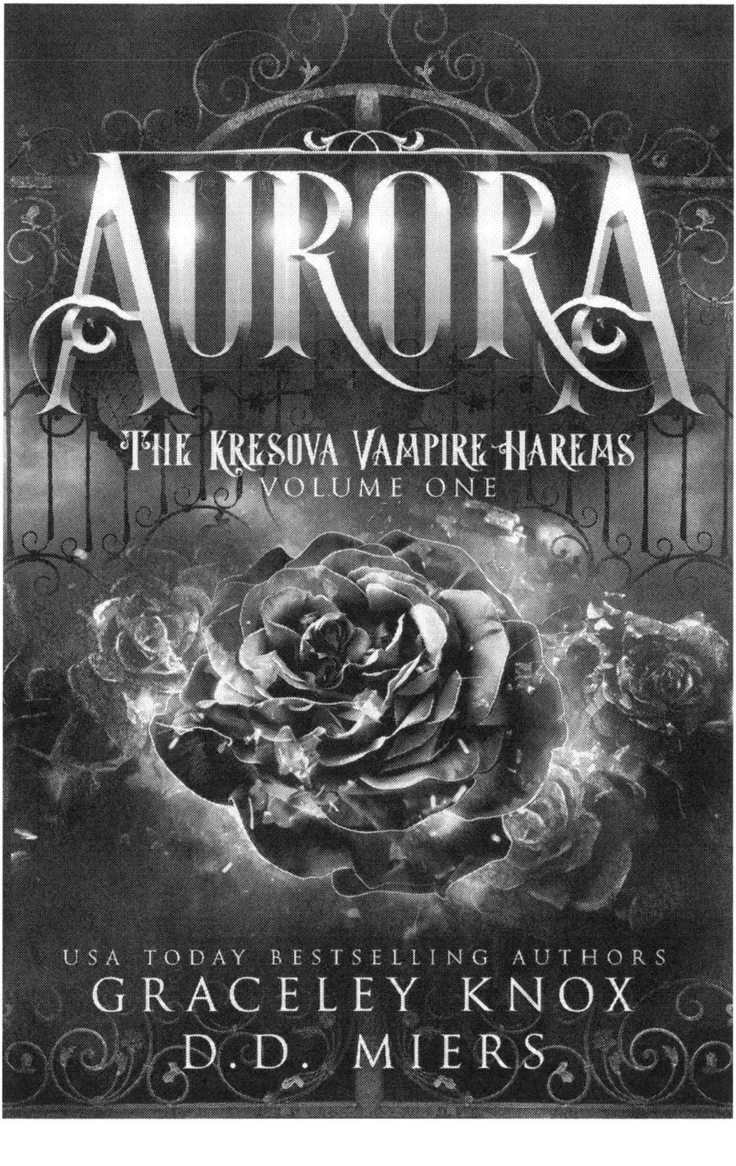
AURORA
THE KRESOVA VAMPIRE HAREMS
VOLUME ONE
USA TODAY BESTSELLING AUTHORS
GRACELEY KNOX
D.D. MIERS

EPIGRAPH

Sometimes, it takes a pawn to dethrone a queen.

THE KRESOVA

Blood.

The source of life—and the emblem of death.

For humans and vampires alike, blood determines the difference between survival or doom. For the ancient race of Kresova vampires, blood spilled in a centuries-old feud has forever changed the course of their future.

Many may know their name, and books may tell their stories, but little truth is actually known about those who stalk the night —especially by the vampires themselves—and the vicious Kresova queen plans to keep it that way.

She kills without prejudice. Eliminates anyone whose existence threatens her rule. Through fear and violence and her unmatched ability to anticipate her enemies, she's secured her reign.

She's thought of everything.

Done everything.

But her plan is flawed.

She didn't prepare for *her* . . . for *them.*

PROLOGUE

The Chamber of Morana, Queen of the Kresova Vampires
Paris, France

Shades of crimson coated the walls of the small coliseum-like room. Smears of blood trailed along the steps like a winding river leading down to the dais. Every few feet, puddles formed in the crevices of the stone floor, staining the white grout a coppery brown.

The tangy scent of iron filled Carvell "Carver" Marceau's nose, and his fangs descended.

He wished he'd eaten before he had arrived, but he never knew what the queen might demand. He doubted she'd ask him to slaughter thirty men—again—simply for her own delight, but he also knew better than to say "never" when referring to Queen Morana's commands.

Many years had passed since his last visit, and he doubted she'd grown in patience or compassion. If she did demand such a thing from him, he'd have no other option but to oblige.

Corpses littered the walkway, sprawled haphazardly with

their throats torn, lying in pools of their own blood. The rubber soles of Carver's sable boots squished and squeaked as though he traversed through a rain-battered street. Rivulets of the thick liquid appeared in each crack that sloped downward toward her enormous marble throne.

At the base of the dais, he stopped. His face, often described by her majesty as regal, remained downturned until she deigned to acknowledge him.

He cast his eyes up, only once, to see she clutched a man in her arms. Her embrace wasn't tender as she pulled at his jugular. When Morana's eyes darted to Carver, she paused, then ferociously tore the man's head from his neck and carelessly dropped his body. It landed with a thud. The crack of human bones shattering echoed throughout the empty throne room.

She kept her gaze fixed on Carver, watching . . . waiting.

For what? Weakness, possibly contempt, but most of all—anything that spoke of treason.

It was a test.

Everything was, when it came to the Kresova queen. But Carver had become a master of self-possession in his long years away from her court, and his expression remained composed. Face still lowered, he waited patiently for her to speak first.

One didn't talk to Queen Morana. Not unless a permanent death was planned. She hadn't maintained her reign over the ancient vampire race of the Kresova this long with kindness and shows of mercy.

Morana's beauty could not be denied, and though she appeared youthful and innocent, she was thousands of years old.

Most of the vampires in existence hadn't been around long enough to remember she was not the first vampire—simply the most cunning.

"Ah, *mon assassin*, you've come to see me at last." Her voice rippled through him like an electric shock to his nerves.

Carver couldn't deny his draw to her. She had sired and

turned him. Their connection would never cease to be until her death—or his.

"Oui, Majesté, I am at your service." He bowed low, his gaze firmly on the blood-stained floor.

"Do you know why I have called you to my side?"

"Non, je ne sais pas, Majesté." No, he wasn't sure why she'd ask for him after a two-hundred-year absence. He'd assumed she'd found a new butcher, as she liked to call him, and moved on from the slight obsession she had formed.

Carver tensed as her slipper-covered feet entered his field of vision. She stood on the upper steps of her throne, keeping herself high above his six-two frame.

"Will you not look upon your queen?" Her blood-soaked hand reached for his chin and brought his face up only inches from hers

Her silver gown had drops of blood over the bodice. Thick liquid dyed the hem a dark gray. He took in her angular face, and their eyes met. Though her wide mouth was still smeared with fresh blood, it didn't diminish the crystal blue of her irises.

He held in a shudder of distaste and kept his expression neutral.

"Ah, that is better, *n'est-ce pas?"* Morana clicked her tongue and stepped back toward her throne.

One of her recent meals lay slumped down into the seat, his blood leaving a puddle on the cushion. With a flick of her wrist, the man flew across the room. He crashed into the wall with a crack, his motionless body broken on the floor.

Carver nodded and waited for her to situate herself before she spoke. The back of his neck tingled as he sensed two bodyguards hidden in the shadows. He didn't need to look to know they scrutinized his every move.

"Now, where were we?" She clasped her hands together in her lap. "Oh, *oui,* I need you to track down the Kresova responsible for turning new members without my permission." A smile lit her pixie-like face.

"Of course, *Majesté.* With whom should I speak to get the details?" He was careful in his wording, his voice steady, sure to include her title.

"Speak with anyone you choose."

"*Oui, Majesté.* Anything else you require?"

A smirk lifted the corners of her mouth, and she tilted her head. She didn't move, but a vampire as old as she, didn't have to. Suddenly, Carver felt the heat of Morona's hand as it caressed down his chest.

Hundreds of years ago, part of Carver's purpose was keeping the queen's carnal appetites satisfied. Even as a human, his stamina and mastery had been something to behold. They'd often referred to him as the Lord of Pleasure.

The gift he possessed had been both his saving grace and his ultimate doom. When the queen of vampires chose someone, there was no walking away.

She stroked the muscles of his stomach, her hands slowly easing down the V of his abdomen to her favorite part of his anatomy. If she asked him to please her again, here and now—whether he wanted to or not—he would.

As quickly as her desire had risen, it dissolved. "*Non.*" Morana waved a hand to dismiss him. "I want this problem gone. *Compris?*"

Carver nodded, already making a mental list of who to talk to. "*Oui, considérez cela comme fait, Majesté.*"

Morana smiled, showing her fangs, then shooed him from her sight.

Carver lowered his head and bowed. He walked backward a few paces, then turned and took the last several steps from her chamber.

When his feet hit the pavement outside Morana's chateau, Carver released the breath he'd been holding. A sweet, creamy vanilla scent enveloped his senses from the wide array of flowers lining her enormous property.

He'd prepared himself to witness her openly vicious behavior, but this new, quiet ferocity had Carver questioning his queen's true plans. She'd never been one to hold back, so why now?

Carver climbed into his Ferrari Enzo, pressed his finger on the button, and the engine growled to life.

Tension bloomed in Carver's chest. Whatever Morana had in store, it was big, and when Morana did big, the body count was always high.

CHAPTER ONE

New Orleans, Louisiana - French Quarter
Mardi Gras, Fat Tuesday

Fuck if I don't go blind.

Neon lights flash against the painted black walls in colors like Crayola on crack. Everywhere I look, light glints from heavy metal chains hanging from leather and faded denim. The reflections cast beams on the floor like a disco ball.

The sweet scent of hookah mingles with cigarettes permeated through the open side door, leaving a smoky film over the crowd. Bodies glisten with sweat as they writhe together on the dance floor. Wrinkle-proof Dockers and pastel-tinged polo shirts grind against flesh marred with piercings, symbols, and obscenities.

This is what I love about the French Quarter.

The vibrant mix of sinners and wannabe saints melds into one delicious pot. Walk the streets on any given day, and you could go from sniffing the most delicious fried beignets to being assaulted by the scent of fresh vomit and human waste. There's no real beauty in perfection—and Louisiana doesn't hide her scars.

That's what drew me here.

I'm a transplant. An outsider who arrived six months ago. In all this time, I've never regretted leaving California.

Not until seven days ago.

I lean back against the bar on my elbows, watching the masses. They move to the heavy beats of the music, heads thrown back in rapture exposing the smooth flesh of their necks.

The simple movement ensnares me.

Getting bitten by a vampire in New Orleans is about as cliché as it got. I can't even say the words out loud without feeling like I've landed in some badly written *Twilight* fanfiction.

Each night, I fall asleep hoping I'll awaken and discover that the crazy shit which transpired just outside of Bourbon Street couldn't have been real.

I've come to the conclusion there are two options: I've been attacked by a psychopath and am now going through some form of toxic blood poisoning clearly affecting my mind, or the vampire was real and now life, or more correctly death, is about to get complicated as hell.

But my heart continues to beat. I draw breath. I want food. All of it. I even walk in the daylight. So, what does this mean?

Fuck, I don't know. I'm still trying to process.

The last two days, nothing but need and want plagues me. I suffer from an insatiable thirst for something I can't understand. A want for satisfaction. Desire. My skin doesn't even feel like my own anymore. I hover over myself, watching helplessly as the pendulum drops.

Is Aurora Hedvige dead? Or do I still exist?

After hours on google researching "vampire transformation," morbid curiosity got the best of me, and I'd indulged the crazy. I drove to the twenty-four-hour market and purchased a package of beef organs soaked in raw blood and a Twinkie so the clerk wouldn't look at me like a total freak.

I took two bites, then forced myself to drink the blood.

Did I get the satisfaction I sought? No, instead I spent the entire night barfing over the toilet with severe stomach cramps.

I'm out of options and about to do the most desperate and ridiculous thing I can do. I came to *The Yowlin' Wolf* looking for answers. Answers only one person can give me. When she's not creating voodoo dolls and selling magic candles to the drunken tourists, Mama Lisette rents the third-floor kitchen for her catering business.

It seems absurd to imagine a woman whose flyers proclaim her the Madame of Black Magic cooking pork shoulder and corn bread with an apron on. But as my best friend Reina says, "Even voodoo queens have to pay their bills."

At the very least, she'll laugh at me. At the very worst, she'll take my money, and I'll see shit for it. All I know is, if Mama Lisette can't help me, my second stop is the emergency room where I'll beg for a psychiatric hold.

What makes tonight so do-or-die?

Plenty. This morning, I lunged for my best friend's throat. She had to fight me off with all her strength, and I still didn't stop. Not until she smacked me over the head with my favorite lamp.

When I finally awoke five minutes later, Reina was crouched on the floor crying. I've never had a propensity for violence, and I'm not about to start.

Coming to see Mama Lisette is Reina's idea. She told me when her boyfriend's ex had gotten out of control, Mama Lisette had helped her create a protection spell which seemingly worked.

Did I believe that? I'm not sure, but I'm also not in the position to be choosy.

A hand taps my forearm, and I turn to see Reina. "Hey, chickadee! Sorry, I'm late." She leans in and gives me a half hug. "How are you feeling?" She flips her long bluish-black hair off her shoulder with her free hand. Reina is your typical gothic girl. She likes skulls, any shade of black, has a sharp tongue—and a hugely hidden heart.

Tonight, she's wearing a tight black dress, which flares at her hips. The material changes from solid to swaths of gossamer material trailing behind her like a train. Her pale arms are covered in fishnets, and her dainty hands are covered by clunky silver rings and bracelets.

No one ever expected the two of us to be acquaintances—let alone best friends. Between my love for pastels and flip-flops, long, blond hair and California beach tan, visually, we scream opposites. Together, we look like a yin-yang symbol.

Even if our conversation isn't secretive, the volume in this place requires us to huddle our heads together and yell.

"Considering everything?" I shrug. "As good as can be. I haven't attacked anyone—yet."

Reina frowns. "We'll figure this out, Aura."

Aura was the nickname Reina had given me when we'd first met.

"I should be the one asking you." I lean back and look at her neck. Faded purple marks, which will likely deepen over the next few days, mar her ivory skin. "Are *you* okay?"

Reina orders a vodka soda from the baby-faced bartender and turns her attention back to me. "I told you, I am."

"And you promise to uphold the plan, right?"

The plan to get me admitted, by force if necessary, if this last-ditch effort didn't pan out.

"I told you I would."

Reina refuses to state whether or not she believes me. Instead, she only claims she believes *I* believe. Whatever the fuck that means.

"Good." I turn my head, and my nose twitches. Tendrils of different smells tantalize me. Desire mixed with sweat and blood formulate the perfect cocktail. The coppery tinge stops my perusal, and I narrow my eyes. Searching. Just as quickly as the scent torments me, it escapes my grasp like a plume of smoke. I continue my search and wrinkle my nose as a strong draft of too much aftershave hits me.

"Aura?"

Reina's concerned eyes study me. "What?"

"I was talking, and you didn't even hear me."

"I'm sorry." I shake my head, "It's getting worse."

"I know." She grabs her glass off the bar and downs it. I think she is feeling less confident than she wants me to believe. "All right, let's do this."

Reina drops a twenty on the bar and starts toward the back hallway.

Two flights up a creaky wooden staircase, a right turn, and we reach the third floor. A scratched-up door sits at the end of the hall and the sounds of Spanish music echo from a window. A white, handwritten piece of paper with the words *Mofongo Mama* is taped to the outside. My stomach growls as the aroma of pan-fried garlic and plantains floats through the frame.

I haven't eaten since the organs incident.

Reina raises her fist to knock, and I catch it with my hand before she touches the wood. "Do you really think this is a good idea? I'm starting to genuinely regret this."

"It will be fine. I promise." She tugs herself free and knocks three times.

Dishes clatter from inside and the music lowers. Footsteps snap against the squeaky floorboards until they stop on the other side of the door. The deadbolt clicks before the door cracks open.

"Yes?" A young girl in her mid-teens with curly brown hair stands on the other side of the threshold.

Reina says, "We're here to see Mama Lisette."

"For?" The girl pivots on her hip, as though she's done it a thousand times.

"My friend here has a problem." Reina grabs my arm and pulls me forward to stand beside her.

The young girl assesses me from my worn converse sneakers to the messy blond bun atop my head. "She only sees clients at her shop on Royal Street. Visit her there on Tuesday."

As the girl moves to close the door, Reina uses her booted foot to wedge it open. "This isn't the sort of situation where we can just 'come back another time.' Please, we need to see her tonight. Now."

"Reina, let's just forget—"

"No. You promised we would try, and right now, you're not even trying."

She's right. I gave up long before we even arrived.

Reina and I have been friends since we met eight years ago. When she moved from Cali to Louisiana, I thought I died inside.

Now, that statement feels far less authentic.

We remained close over the years, and as soon as I finished my two years at JC, I packed up my things and moved here.

We've never faced a problem without each other. When her neglectful mother died and left her their house, we'd moved in and made it our own. Now, I'm apparently a bloodsucker, and we're here together, facing that as well.

I take a deep breath and look straight into the young girl's big, brown eyes. "Look, just tell her something for me—and if she still doesn't want to see us—then we'll go."

"And what do you want me to tell her?"

God, I can't believe I'm saying this out loud. "I think I was bitten by a vampire. I crave something I can't discern, and I tried to attack her this morning." I gesture to Reina.

Surprisingly, the girl doesn't laugh or even smile. She leans her head to the side, keeping her gaze on mine. The throb of her jugular captures my attention, and I can't look away.

"Wait here." She snaps the door shut. A minute later, she returns holding the door open, ushering us inside. As we slip into the entryway, she stops. "You'll need to take off your shoes. Mama doesn't like the soils from outside brought in."

I lean one hand on the wall and kick off my converse shoes. Reina does the same with her boots. It feels strange to enter her home without knowing her name. I introduce myself. "I'm Aurora by the way, and she's Reina"

"Breanne." The girl nods. "You brought money?"

Reina pulls a wad of cash out of her purse and pulls two hundred-dollar bills. She places them in Breanne's palm.

Breanne doesn't say anything. She takes the money and turns. I can't tell whether she's always like this or she doesn't like me. Her bare feet pad down the hall ahead of us. I assume we're supposed to follow, so we do. We pass several bedrooms and an arched doorframe which gives us a peek into a soft yellow-and-white kitchen. I can't see the stove, but the aromas floating around are revving my appetite again.

At the end of the hall, the space opens up to a large living room with high tray ceilings. A small TV hums in the corner, the barely audible sounds of a reality show competing with the low music playing from another room. This apartment appears aged and worn but not unappealing. A sea-green recliner faces the television, and the back of a woman's curly red-haired head perches over the top cushion.

Breanne walks up to her and whispers something into the woman's ear. She picks up a remote from the end table, clicks the TV off, and spins around.

I'm shocked to see that Mama Lisette is barely older than us, maybe late twenties at the most. Her strawberry blond hair falls in curls around her tan, heart-shaped face. She looks so different from the flyers. I imagine she must wear lots of makeup and a wig when she's playing the Madame of Black Magic.

"So, which one of you needs my help?"

I raise my hand slightly and smile. I've never felt more

ridiculous in my life, but since no one else is laughing, I won't either.

She keeps her eyes fixed on me. "You were bitten?"

"I'm pretty sure."

"You either were—or you weren't—so which is it?"

This chick isn't fucking around.

I know it happened, but the longer I doubt it, the longer I have before everything in my life changes. "I was."

The cushion creeks as she stands and takes three steps toward me. "Where?"

This is the awkward part. He'd bitten me just over my left breast. I have to tug down the neck of my blouse to show her. "Here," I say, revealing the torn flesh.

The wound has yet to heal. If anything, it looks worse today than when it happened. Two red, angry bite marks surrounded by blue-green bruises and several other teeth indents.

She doesn't ask my permission as she traces her hand over my wound and then pauses. "I need you to sit down." She drops down to her knees before me as I land on the couch cushion. She returns her hand to my skin and closes her eyes. Her lips move, but no sound comes out.

No, this isn't awkward at all. There's just a voodoo queen holding my breast in her palm while she chants to herself.

I glance over to Reina. She smiles, encouraging me to stick with this even though I'm clearly not feeling it. Just when I'm starting to think this is a load of bullshit, everything in the room fades, and I'm thrust into a storm.

The world moves at an impossible pace of both slow motion and fast forward. Time lurches, and I'm back at work last week. My coworker, Ashley, drops her pen into the mocha she just bought. It splashes up and whipped cream hits her glasses. We both start laughing.

Time zooms again, and now I'm standing at the door of my car. It's evening, and low fog has rolled in. I pluck my keys from my purse. Seconds later, a hand grabs me from behind. I drop my keys and scream, and time moves again.

I'm being slammed against a grime-covered wall between two buildings. Another flash and the stench of rotten garbage and something I can't discern, something . . . metallic? My chest burns, and I open my eyes. I'm slumped against the wall as a man is biting into the top of my breast. I want to fight, but I can't. I feel the strength leaving me.

White light flashes, and now I am standing in a blood-covered room. No, not a room, a chamber. Bodies litter the floor as a sea of ruby flows from the ground. A woman sits on a stone throne. She raises a finger toward me, and as something flies from her hands, time zooms once more.

I stand before a man. Everything about him is in shadow except the piercing blue of his eyes. He turns away, and a door slams shut in my face, an enormous K engraved on it.

"Aura! Aura!"

I open my eyes and see Reina and Breanne leaning over me. I'm flat on my back, covered in layers of sweat. "What the fuck?" I say as I sit up. My head spins from moving too quickly.

"What the fuck is right." Reina turns from me to Mama Lisette who's crouched on her hands and knees several feet away. "What the hell did you do to her?"

"What happened?" I ask.

"You had a seizure or something. It's been almost ten-freakin'-minutes, and nobody here would let me call for help."

Reina's pissed. Breanne watches us both, and Mama Lisette stares at me like I'm a two-headed unicorn. At that moment, I realize she's also covered in sweat and shaking. Did she see all of that? Did she feel it?

"I can't help you," Mama Lisette says as she climbs to her feet. "You need to go."

With Reina's help, I stand. "What just happened to me? Why do you look so scared?"

She shakes her head and moves toward the kitchen, but I follow. I grab her arm. She tries to tug herself free, but my grip is too strong.

It's *never* been this strong.

We both look down at my hand, and after a second, I release her. "You said you could help."

"I never said that I could. I only asked who needed help and what happened."

"Then why did you let us in?"

She shakes her head again, and I hear Reina and Breanne come in behind me.

"I can't help unless—"

"Unless what?" Reina snaps. "Unless we give you another five hundred dollars? Is that what this is? A shakedown?"

Mama Lisette slams her fits onto the counter. "Unless the vampire is still alive!" Her hand points to me as if in accusation. "But your sire is dead. Of that much, I am certain. There's no way to stop the change now."

"Holy fuck." Reina practically falls into a chair beside her. "This is real?"

A million questions rush my mind, but I can't formulate words. The sight of all that blood is doing something to me. My skin itches and aches at the same time, and a ravenous hunger, one I've tried to bury deep, has surged to the forefront of my thoughts.

"You're at the end of this, Aurora. I'm surprised you haven't already succumbed."

Reina looks from me to Mama Lisette before she speaks. "How long does she have?"

Mama shrugs. "Hours. Minutes? I've never seen someone go as long as she has without turning." She nudges her head toward me. "You're running on empty, Aurora. It will only take one moment." She snaps her fingers. "Then your control will disappear."

"Can't you give her something, to help?" Reina asks. "Cast a protection spell on her mind? Or something? Anything!"

Reina's desperation shocks me out of my thoughts.

Mama Lisette shakes her head, "This is different."

"Why?" I ask.

"You know why."

"No, I don't."

"You saw it too, Aurora. You felt it."

Reina grabs my bicep. "Saw what, Aura?"

"This kind of magic, this kind of power, it's connected to something dark. Something ancient." Mama steps toward me and places her hands on my shoulders. "The darkness is coming for you, Aurora. You can't outrun it. You can't hide from it. And you can't defeat it."

"What are you saying?" Reina asks.

Mama doesn't move her eyes from mine. "I'm saying Aurora is marked by death—and her time has run out."

DEAR READER,

Thank you so much for taking the time to read *Girl, Immortal.* We hope you enjoyed reading about Sasha through the Girl, Vampire Trilogy!

If you enjoyed *Girl, Immortal,* please consider leaving a review on Amazon or Goodreads. We love any and all feedback and every review counts!

If you'd like to be notified of upcoming releases, giveaways, and more, sign up for our newsletter, here!

Stay Wicked,

Graceley & Dee

ALSO BY GRACELEY KNOX & D.D. MIERS

The Kresova Vampire Harems: Aurora (Written with D.D. Miers)

1. Thirst

2. Tempt

3. Turn

Aurora Books 1-3

The Kresova Vampire Harems: Lyra (Written with D.D. Miers)

4. Favor

5. Fury

The Girl, Vampire Series

1. Girl, Bitten

2. Girl, Forsaken

3. Girl, Immortal

The Half-Blood Huntress Chronicles

Prequel: Deck the Demons (Exclusively in Such Violent Delights)

1. Curse of Iron

2. Heir of Storm

3. Master of Magic

4. Reign of Rebels

5. War of Thrones

How to Date A Supernatural

1. How to Date a Werewolf… or 3

2. How to Capture a Demon's Heart

The Shadow Creatures Series

1. Gravestones & Wicked Bones

2. Cursed Moons & Ancient Runes (Coming 2019!)

How to Be A Necromancer

1. *Grave Promise*

2. *Grave Debt*

3. Grave Mistake

4. Grave Magic

5. Grave Chance

Alana Creed: Timejumper

1. *Fae Kissed*

By Graceley Knox

The Wicked Kingdoms Series:

1. Mark of Truth

2. Crown of Betrayal

3. Throne of Secrets

3.5. Yuletide Revelry (A Wicked Kingdoms Christmas Short)

4. Castle of Illusions

The Dragon Charm Saga:

Kiss of Frost

Up in Smoke (Coming Soon)

Shake the Ground (Coming Soon)

By D.D. Miers

The Relic Keeper Series

1. *Dark Summoner*

2. *Dark Illusions*

3. *Dark Secrets* (Coming Soon!)

4. *Dark Destiny* (Coming Soon!)

The Supernaturals of Los Melas

1. *Gretel: Witch Hunter*

Standalones:

City of Shadows: The Dark Fae Hollows

Wicked: The Isa Fae

Slayer in Lace

ABOUT THE AUTHORS

USA Today bestselling authors, Graceley Knox and D.D. Miers may be long-lost sisters, but their moms continue to deny it. They are most definitely the co-writers of the Kresova Vampire Harem series, as well as a multitude of other upcoming projects they can't wait to share with readers.

Together they tend to share the same brain, finish each other's thoughts, laugh way too hard at inappropriate comments, drink enough coffee to qualify for an intervention, and talk about their fur babies. When they're not chatting, which is always, they can be found all over social media hanging out with their author friends and readers!

Visit them at www.knoxandmiers.com
Sign up for their Newsletter here!

Made in the USA
Columbia, SC
25 January 2023

11090692R00126